All Good Men Must Fall

My Temporary Life Book Three

by

Martin Crosbie

All Good Men Must Fall

My Temporary Life Book Three

Copyright 2017 Martin Crosbie.

ISBN: 09921128-8-2

ISBN – 13: 978-0-9921128-8-2

Chapter One

THERE'S A NOISE *in the hallway. It's not right outside the door, but it's close. It sounds like it's coming from the top of the stairs, the opposite end from where Emily's room is. Malcolm is at Hardly's. Flora left again and he's afraid Hardly might be into the booze. He says he isn't, but we're not sure we believe him. So Malcolm will talk Hardly down and then fall asleep on their couch, just like he did last time.*

Again. I hear it again. It's like coins slowly being shaken back and forth, in a jar. It sounds like a glass jar. I lift my head up from the pillow and lean on my elbow to hear it better. It's stopped. I can't hear it now. It wasn't an old house groaning at night type of sound, and this is an old house; it was built before the war. That's what the Scottish people say. The timeline is always things that happened before the war or things that happened after the war. Yes, the war that ended in nineteen forty-five, that war. It's been over for more than fifty years. We're two years into the new century – it's 2002, but the older Scots still refer to things as before the war or after the war. Like it just ended.

Again. Damn.

I sit up and pull the covers around me. The coins shake three, four times and then stop. No, this isn't one of those hard-to-explain creaks that you get from an old house. This is too real, too vibrant.

It stops again. I wait and wait. I can hear the sound of my breathing. The noisiest thing in the whole house is the sound of my own breathing. Nothing happens. It's my imagination. It has to be. I pull the covers tighter around me, and the jangling noise starts again. It's louder now. What is it? What is it?

"Em. Emily, honey."

She sleeps like a log these days.

"Emily, can you hear that?" She won't hear me. She's fifteen and retreating, leaving us for classmates who know more than we do.

Something moves down the hallway past my door toward Emily's room. The coins are jangling as it rolls past. "No. No. No." I raise my voice. I'm not screaming. I won't scream. I won't give him the satisfaction.

I'm out of bed and into the hall. Why is it so dark? All the downstairs lights are off. I know I left a light on.

"Malcolm, are you down there?"

It's too dark. I can't see, but I know something's here.

Emily's door opens slowly and a little bit of light trickles out. Shit. Shit.

"Mom, what is it?" She's rubbing at the sleep in her eyes, looking at me, angry, bewildered.

"Did you hear it? Something rolled down the hall. Where is it?" I look up and down. The light from Emily's room lights up the floor, the hallway, all the way to the landing. There's nothing here but I know I heard it. The noise from the jar and the coins shaking around is still clear in my head. I know it was here. It was outside my door. I pace up and down the hallway, keeping my back against the wall. All I see are a couple of dust bunnies rolling around on the wood floor.

"You're sweating, Mom. What did you hear?"

She's right. I touch my forehead with my fingers. It's cold sweat. "I'm okay. I just thought I heard something. I'm going to call Malcolm; he's at Uncle Harry's."

"I know. You told me already." Just a hint of indignation. I'll take it; it doesn't matter.

"Okay, go back to bed."

She waits, weighing the choice between the warmth of her bed or placating her crazy mother. She decides to take pity on me. "I'll wait up with you in your room, and if the noises start again we'll phone Dad."

She doesn't always call him that, he's usually Malcolm. She's scared, too. She might not have heard it but she knows I did.

"It's gone, Mom. Nothing was here and now it's gone."

She's wrong. It's not gone. Ghosts are everywhere. They're always here. We think they're gone. We think they died on snowy highways, in another country, in a different life but they're still here. We think we can start a new life and adjust our story to suit ourselves. We think that ghosts just disappear but sometimes they don't.

She takes my hand and leads me down the hallway and flicks on the light at the top of the stairs, the same light I left on earlier. It's quiet now. There are no noises. She looks at me and smiles that everything will be alright. Maybe she's right. Maybe it will. I was probably just hearing noises again. This isn't the first time this has happened.

Chapter Two

THERE'S A SMALL Asian man who stands on the corner of the High street. He wears a sign, a placard that reads, "Repent, Jesus Is Coming." From time to time, someone yells at him from their open car window, telling him to get a job or go find Jesus somewhere else. It flusters him and he calls back, angrily warning them of their sins, both real and imagined. Even though I was born here it still amazes me that an Asian man can have a Scottish accent. In his Kilmarnock brogue, he'll call out to the occupant of the car who tried to offend him and tell him that Jesus is coming for their arse and they better watch themselves. Sometimes, as the cars pass by, a hand will reach out a window and two fingers point upwards giving the Asian man that unique, profane Scottish salute. The man doesn't care. He's out there in all weather, and if it rains he wears an old-fashioned, triangular rain hat that he's pulled onto his head incorrectly. A side flaps down on the front and back and the hat is tied around the side of his head.

During the first few months after we arrived in Scotland, we'd slow down occasionally and speak to him. Emily would be in the back and Heather and she would struggle to understand the man's choppy, Scottish accent. Inevitably, it would be raining and Heather would make me steer over to the side of the road while she put her window down to ask the man if he was doing okay.

"I'm right as rain, hen. God bless you for stopping."

I smile and nod, anxious to move us along. If it were just Heather and I we'd be able to continue but the times we have Emily with us we're stuck. She's enchanted by his accent and sees him as some sort of amusement. At first, she leans back in her seat smiling at him, but after a couple of times she becomes braver and slouches forward, her head pressing against the back of her mother's seat. She smirks at the man as he stands there.

"You need to go inside; you're getting too wet."

Heather has frightened her with tales of the torrential Scottish rains. I think Emily feels as though the man is going to be washed away.

"You're American. You're a wee American girl."

A horn sounds behind me and before the driver can deliver the Scottish salute I say good day to the biblical repenter and drive us back into the traffic. Emily turns in her seat and calls back to him as we pull away.

"I'm not American. I'm Canadian."

We'd been in Scotland for six months. That was during the good times. My father immediately took to Heather, and in his traditional Scottish way, he pretended we were married. With his crinkled smile he calls her my wife. I even find myself doing the same once in a while. And, he tells us that Emily is more of a Scot than I am and calls her his wee Scottish bisem – a rascal. When she hears the name, she runs at him and smacks her open hands on his chest. It's as though she's always been waiting to have him in her life and when he appeared, he filled that void for her. It felt natural to all of us. She became closest to my friend Hardly, though. When we moved here her ten-year-old ears couldn't decipher his Scottish accent and instead of calling him Uncle Hardly he became Uncle Harry to her, and only to her. There were days when Emily and her Uncle Harry were inseparable.

When we return from our errands Emily insists that we loop around the block and pass the man once more even though it means doubling back once we've driven past him on the other side of the street. She makes me pull the car close to him. When he's beside us, she leans forward and calls through Heather's half-open window.

"I'm Scottish now, not American or Canadian."

And that's how we knew. It was as simple as that. We knew she was probably going to be okay. After everything that had happened, moving her from her home, explaining to her that the man who raised her was dead, and introducing her to Heather and explaining that she was her birth mother had all been so much for one little girl, but in that moment we knew she'd decided to try. I didn't look at Emily and Heather kept staring straight ahead, but we both heard it. We made our way off the high street and over to Longpark, and then home. Heather reached her hand back over her shoulder and after a moment Emily took it.

Scotland was our safe haven. That's why we stayed. Canada represented all the bad things. I left friends back there, and my business, too, but we had no choice. We didn't want to think about what happened, analyze it, or re-visit it. We just wanted to start over. When we first arrived, we rented a house. Hardly, my old childhood friend, moved with his girlfriend Flora into a house across the street and my dad lived in the same neighborhood, a ten-minute walk away. It was perfect. We had the support system when we needed it and we had our privacy, too. The Kilmarnock of my youth, the one that isolated me in my bedroom and made me climb up trees and hide, was more welcoming this time. My fears were gone and it felt like the town had grown up while I was away in Canada growing up myself. I'd left at fifteen and returned briefly in my early twenties when I graduated from college. Now as an almost forty-year-old man, I'd experienced too much to have a town full of youthful memories stand in the way of living the life I was meant to live.

When I received the proceeds from the sale of my business to my partners in Canada, we made a generous offer to our landlord and

7

bought our old, rented house. Heather reluctantly accepted some money from her father's estate that she contributed to the sale, and we had enough money to begin figuring out what our life in Scotland was going to look like. The days found their own rhythm and all the details began to fall into place. Once the paperwork was complete, we wanted to make the house feel like our own so we made some changes. Heather picked up a used sewing machine at a jumble sale and made curtains from brightly colored material that she bought at a charity shop. And she made a cover for the old chair in the living room that she insisted on keeping. We bought furniture and delivered it using a truck, or lorry, as the Scots call them, that Hardly borrowed from an old Army friend, and within a couple of weeks, it felt like a home. Our home.

Our life was new, and full of promise. Heather had her dark times but mostly she had good days, manageable days. She'd sit in the old armchair sewing, and the light from the front window would stream in. I'd always smile at her when I walked into that room.

"If you're going to say something rude, I advise you to re-think, Malcolm."

"Not rude at all. It's beautiful; I like what you're doing." The light settles peacefully on her shoulders. I get one of those pangs in my heart and it takes me back to another time. I remember our camping trip to the lake at the end of the world. "The house feels warm; it's nice. You should know, though, this is probably the hottest you'll ever be in this country. It never really heats up here. It's always cold."

She answers right away, without hesitation. "I don't care. It doesn't matter."

She's changing. She's not the confident woman who I couldn't stop thinking about and she's not the scared girl who used to run away from her problems, either. There's something different now. It's like she's trying to find her feet again. I squeeze her hand as I leave the room and it's still there. I feel the electricity running through my body, the same way it did when I first touched her. She smiles back at me and then goes back to her sewing.

Hardly and I painted walls. We left the walls in his rented house for his landlord to redecorate, but we painted every room in the house that Heather and I bought. We asked Emily what color she preferred for her bedroom. We showed her samples and expected her to pick a girlish pink, or perhaps a purple.

"That one and that one." She pointed her finger to a bright shade of orange and a vibrant blue then looked at me and then to Hardly.

My accent was still Canadian in those days and hadn't reverted back to Scottish so I wasn't a novelty to her but my friend was and it was to him whom she listened.

"Are you sure, love? Do you not want something a wee bit more girly?"

"Those are my colors, Uncle Harry. Sky colors."

So we painted Emily's room the colors of her sky, orange and blue.

As a child, I visited my share of local historical sites. Some I'd gone to on school trips or occasionally my proud, amateur-historian father would take me out for the day. If they ever held any type of fascination, that had long disappeared, but in this second incarnation, it seemed appropriate to show off the country of my birth and its history. Heather had interested Emily in standing stones, the ancient, mysterious erections that are said to hold spiritual significance. On weekends, we would travel up and down the motorways, pulling off at small towns and walking into farmer's fields where the stones are left for all to see. Sometimes my dad would join us, or Hardly and Flora would come along, and those were good days, but the times when it was just the three of us were often the most special.

We pull into the village with the unlikely name of Dailly, a few miles from our home in Kilmarnock. Emily takes her wellington boots from the boot of the car. They're a size too big and flop around as she walks.

She's in front of us and Heather calls out as she trudges over the dirt toward the stones. "Em, are you sure you don't want to wear your runners? You might slide and fall in those."

Even though she wasn't born here, she's taken to everything Scottish including the tall, cumbersome rubber boots. "Nope. I like them."

Heather smiles at me and I put my arm around her as we walk behind Emily. There's a man in the distance bending over a piece of farm machinery and he waves to us when we reach the stones.

"Thank you," Heather calls out to him.

He stands up and stretches himself. He looks over in our direction and I can't tell if he's grimacing or smiling. For a moment he looks like he's going to make his way toward us.

I speak in a low voice. "Please no. Don't come. I don't need to hear your story."

Heather nudges me in the ribs and thankfully the man picks up a tool and just waves at us.

Emily has her arms folded and is looking at the stones as though she may derive some type of energy from them. Heather laughs as she playfully scolds me.

"Why do you do that? He saw your scowl and probably decided to stay where he was. Big, brooding Scottish boy scaring off the farmer."

"I know. I just don't need to have another one of those guys telling me how they have to leave the path clear so that we can come and look at the stones. We know that already; that's why we're here."

"Shhh." Emily has her finger on her lips and her other little hand waves at us to be quiet. "I think I feel something."

The sun is at our backs and I have my family beside me. There are four stones and they're arranged in a circular pattern. The years have worn away what were once probably even edges and now the tops are ragged. They're mounted into the ground and stand almost four feet high, slightly taller than Emily. There is a power. I don't know if it's coming from the stones or the sunshine or the feelings I have for the little girl on one side of me and the woman on the other, but it's there. I steal my gaze away from the small structure and look over at Heather. She can't stop staring at Emily. She's smiling and when I reach out for her hand, she takes it without looking away. She squeezes back tight as she loops her hand inside my pinky finger in the special way we've developed of holding onto each other. After a few minutes, Emily looks at us and smiles at her mother.

"We can go now. The spirits say we're going to be okay."

Heather holds out her other hand and without hesitation, Emily comes around beside us and takes it. It's happening quicker now; it's almost natural. When we reach our vehicle, the farmer is nowhere to be seen but sitting on the hood is a brown, paper bag. When I open it there are several neeps or turnips inside. Heather holds it up and looks around, scanning the area for the farmer.

"Malcolm, if you say anything cruel, you'll be eating turnips for a month. One whole month, Malcolm, it's your decision."

I keep my objections to myself and when I look down at Emily. She has her hand over her mouth stifling a laugh. We get into the car and back out of the long, narrow driveway. It's not until we're safely down the road that Emily speaks.

"You like them, though, don't you, Malcolm? You like turnips, I mean neeps."

"Emily." I raise my voice playfully at her.

"Yes, Malcolm." She has the same innocent tone that any little girl might have, but on her, after all she's been through, it means more.

I launch into my newly rediscovered Scots accent when I answer her. "You know very well that I do not like neeps. I grew up on those things and now that I'm an adult I choose to not eat them."

"You're going to though, Malcolm. Aren't you? You're going to eat them." She says with her little-girl, innocent voice, gently poking me in the back of the head from the rear seat.

"No, I'm not."

Then, I'm outgunned as the two of them answer in unison. "Yes, you are, Malcolm."

Every day should be today. Every day should feel like this and everybody in the world should get to experience this feeling every single day. Then nothing would ever go wrong.

Scotland was wonderful for the first couple of years. Emily grew up in the town that I couldn't wait to get out of. She was only a child when we arrived at the airport but she adjusted quickly to the Scots way of life. She was still Heather's little girl in those days, a little girl who'd had too many bad things happen to her but somehow managed to recover. It's strange to think of how well things were going and how everything changed so quickly, but there's a turning point for everything I suppose. I'm not sure exactly when ours happened. It could have been when Hardly began drinking again, or Flora leaving him over and over, or it might have been the ghosts. I don't know what it was. Sometimes you notice the turning points and sometimes they're so subtle that you miss them. I missed ours, whatever it was. I was probably looking too far ahead, thinking that everything was going to last forever. It never has for me though. Everything that happens, whether it's good or bad, has always been temporary.

Chapter Three

MY BEST FRIEND, Gerald McDougall, earned the nickname "Hardly" when we attended primary school together. That's when his addiction to alcohol began. When the teacher asked him one day whether he'd been drinking, he answered "hardly" and the class rechristened him. From that point on the only person I ever heard referring to him as "Gerald" was my father. To the rest of the world he was Hardly.

My friend changed in the years since I'd last seen him. He went from being the little boy who would stare back, not caring what happened to him, to the man who would step up and fight. He had the same sullen defiance about him that he'd had as a youth, but he developed a retaliatory stance that was never there before. He didn't look for trouble but he didn't shy away from it, either. He was no longer the boy who took beatings from his mother and father. He was a different man. I guess that's what happens when you become a soldier and lose part of your leg on the battlefield.

He told me a story about when he was first in the service and spending lots of time at a pub not far from base. He met a woman, a married woman, and they carried on an affair for a few months while her husband was out of town. He talked about it being a rite of passage but I know my mate. I know he regretted the hurt he caused.

I could see it in his eyes when he talked about the husband and how panicked the man looked when he came home to find Hardly in bed with his wife.

"But you knew it might happen one day? It was inevitable that he'd find out."

He's only had a couple of beers, and when he answers he's still clear and stares back, the same way he used to when we were young boys. "Inevitable? Definitely. I think I willed it actually."

He laughs, reliving it I suppose.

"I think for some of us we actually have to make the mistake before we figure out where the line in the sand is. The rest of you lot instinctively know the difference between right and wrong. I'm not so sure I did."

I don't agree with him but I let it go.

"Did you ever see them again?"

He answers right away. "I hear they're doing just fine. I was a minor distraction for a while. They got over it."

We're waiting for Flora, his girlfriend, the one who doesn't always come home. We look out the front window of his living room, and I watch my own house across the street. It's windy and an object that looks like a rolled up piece of paper is blowing down the road from streetlight to streetlight. Hardly is sitting on the edge of the easy chair and I'm on the couch. There's a narrow coffee table in front of us with two mugs and a pot of tea. The volume is set low on his stereo system as the muted sounds of an angry punk rocker stab at the quietness of the house. He has the bass set too high, just the way he likes it.

"I should know who this is but I don't remember his name. The sound is too distorted. Is it the Irish guy again? The one who always sounds like he's drunk?"

He nods and smiles without looking at me. It's a game we play. "You know damn well who it is. Yes, it's the drunken Irishman. He's a poet, really. And, I like the sound just the way it is, it keeps me calm."

I shake my head at him. "I like something a bit more optimistic."

"I know, you like to hear about American girls, and cars, and faded dungarees."

"They're called blue jeans, and I wasn't in America. It was Canada, remember. It was Canadian girls that I met."

I made him smile, just for a moment. He picks up one of the worn, old mugs and looks outside again. It's as though we both just realized that it's been dark for quite some time.

"I should phone her again."

He's no sooner dialed the number when he leaves the message. It's gone straight to her voice mail. He leaves a sweet message quietly imploring her to come back and furnishing her with excuses that she probably won't listen to.

"She's forgotten the time again. She does that. You know that, Malcolm."

"I know she does, Hardly."

Hardly and Flora moved back to the street at the same time Heather, Emily, and I arrived from Canada but they never seemed to gel. He met her when he was serving in Northern Ireland and she came back with him. They both saw a lot of bad stuff over there, more than either of them will talk about. Hardly wants to forget it and move on but there's always something that seems to draw Flora away. She goes out with her girlfriends and disappears for days and nights while Hardly sits and frets. Or, she goes up north, to Aberdeen to see family and stays away longer than planned. We live our lives while our front windows face each other across the street – separate but together. We know more about each other's lives than we probably have a right to.

Emily has settled into her new school. She's moved from primary school to the high school now and made some friends. Heather is still trying to find her way, and some days are better than others. She volunteered at the primary school while Emily attended and stayed on after she moved. She has a paid position now as a teaching assistant, and for a long time all she could speak of was the assistant headmaster, Barry. Barry had opinions and advice that she'd bring home to our house. Then, a few months ago, she stopped speaking about Barry. It doesn't make me jealous, that doesn't happen to me, but it does cause me to worry a little bit.

Hardly sips his tea. His eyebrows burrow together, and he lets out a long sigh. Somewhere in there is the little boy who I used to walk to school with. It seems like it was so long ago. We were both poor, but everybody was poor in those days. I had my dad while Hardly had no support at home. That's why he relied on the alcohol to escape from it all. He was always smaller, shorter than the rest of us and his parents took their own personal frustrations out on him. Not everyone saw it or acknowledged it, but there were days when he came to school covered in bruises. At ten, eleven years of age, I saw the bruises on my friend, but I didn't know what to do about it. My dad did, though. He took him in, helped him to stop drinking, and probably saved his life. Then, when he was old enough, he joined the army and was sent to Northern Ireland. And then it started again – his ongoing battle with the bottle. We're lucky; my dad is still here, for both of us. We all gave up on Hardly's parents a long time ago. His mother died a few years ago and I don't think he's had any contact with his father in years. He's got us now, though.

He's beginning to look sleepy. I'm lucky; I can function on just a few hours each night, unlike the rest of the world. He feels it, though and I know he snuck a couple of drinks earlier in the day. He lets out a yawn and holds his mouth open for a moment. I think he's going to be okay. He's resigned to the fact that he'll spend another night at the window, listening to his music, and wishing things could be different.

"I can't stay here tonight. Heather and Emily are worried. They hear noises in the house."

He sits upright, suddenly wide awake. "Em is scared now? What's going on? The house is blethering in the night again?"

"It's Heather who's worried, not Emily. It's the same things. She thinks she hears something creaking in the hallway. I should go."

He nods, accepting. "Go. Go. I'm fine, Malcolm. I'll be fine."

From his front window, I can see our house across the street, the light in our upstairs bedroom, and a lamp left on in the living room. There's a flicker in the hall as though someone got up to go to the bathroom and then changed their mind. I turn back to my friend before I leave him.

"Don't drink any more, mate. It's not worth it. I'm right over there, remember."

"Go. I'll be fine. And if you need a hand, give me a bell and I'll be right there."

I slap him on the shoulder and make my way across the street. He's different from when we were kids. In those days we avoided confrontation and aggravation. Now, even with his injury, his artificial leg, he's the first man on the scene. My dad was bullied by some young boys a couple of years after we moved back. We knew who they were. They may have changed the name of Craigmore Avenue but the same families still live there. My dad recognized one of the boys. They'd bumped into him as he was walking home from the bus stop and his newspaper had fallen from under his arm. They picked up the paper and jeered at him, running backward and taking his newspaper with them. It was harmless but when it's your father it's different. You make it right. Hardly had been at our house and my dad reluctantly told the story when we asked him where his paper was. Five years earlier the boys would have been limping home after a confrontation with Alex Wilson but my dad seemed to be getting old before his time, and those days had passed. Hardly was first on his feet, his eyes on fire, grabbing his cane and marching to the door.

"Right, Malcolm, let's sort it."

I agree and follow him.

My dad isn't acting like himself, and his reaction puzzles me. "Leave it, Malcolm, both of you, leave it. They're harmless."

He's a changed man from the neighborhood protector that I remember from my childhood. Not so many years earlier, he would have been the first one to react. Hardly stands at the door waiting and ignoring my dad. After watching him settle into his chair I noticed how his face has softened and his features have fallen into place. He's far too ready to dismiss the situation. That wasn't the way he brought me up. I put my hand on his shoulder as I pass him on my way to the door.

Heather questions it and asks what's happening. Hardly explains it to her the only way he knew how.

"We're fixing it, Scottish style, Heather. No worries."

I give her a sheepish smile and close the door behind us.

We walk a couple of streets over and see them right away. They're still laughing, sitting on a small wall outside one of their homes. There are three of them, sixteen, maybe seventeen-year-olds, and there's no newspaper in sight. None of the three moves when they see us coming but the boy on the end flinches. He's the biggest lad. The three of them look tougher and stronger than what we dealt with when we attended the same school that they do.

Hardly may have been a small man but the military made him larger. Even as he leans on his cane, he doesn't back down from anyone anymore. "Right lads, either go get your old man, pay for the newspaper, or you're going to get a battering. It's your choice."

The mouthpiece on the far end laughs while the bigger lad eyes us up, deciding. The one in the middle is either ready to run or he's eyeing up the territory looking for a stick or a bit of pipe that he can use on us.

I recognize the biggest boy. He's the spitting image of one of the boys who used to try and intimidate me. "You're a McGill. I remember your dad. Go get him if you like. You boys took my dad's newspaper earlier. I want the money for it and I don't want to wait. Go get your old man."

Mouthpiece rattles on denying, making up stories about where they'd been all afternoon and that it couldn't have been them. His lies have a sing-song rhythm to them. If only he knew that we've heard them hundreds of times before. The big man speaks right over him.

"We didnae ken it was your old man. We were just mucking about."

"I know that. We did the same things. Now go get your dad or pay the cost of the paper."

He smiles, and even mouthpiece shuts up. He's either going to come off that wall and hit me hard or he's going to do the right thing. I clench my fist in anticipation and wonder how strong a young, fit boy who scraped his way up the worst streets of Kilmarnock is going to be. He shifts a little on the wall, toying with us and Hardly smiles back as though he's getting ready to react, too. Then, he speaks to the middle boy, the one who looks the shiftiest.

"Pay him. Pay him out of the money. Don't argue. Just pay him. He's a neighbor. We don't want to pish on our neighbors."

They've been up to some trouble. The boy takes a small roll of bills from his pocket and peels one off and hands it to Hardly. He grabs it while the mouthpiece shakes his head, trying to argue with the big man.

"Is your dad all right, then?" asks the big boy.

"He's fine. He knows the score. Say hello to your father from me?"

"Aye, I will. C'moan."

He gets up off the wall. The other two instinctively follow him as they're off to raise some kind of havoc with someone else. Hardly nods at me and we make our way back to our house. They won't steer clear of him next time. They'll talk to him in mockingly polite voices, but they won't touch him again. It sent a message. They were told and they understood.

I involuntarily shiver from the cold. When I reach our house both locks are bolted. I sit in the living room and watch across the street. I can vaguely see the outline of my friend sitting at his window, worrying. I think about what he told me about his affair and wonder if this is how life is supposed to feel. Do you have a little place in your heart where you keep your regrets? Do you keep them separate from everything else just so you can survive? I had no justifiable reason to do what I did. Hardly told me the story of his promiscuity with the married woman and he was right. I knew the difference between right and wrong. I would never have asked Heather whether something was going on with Barry and her. I knew the way she spoke about him that they'd become friends and when I asked her why she didn't talk about him any longer, she shrugged it off telling me that it was work stuff and would be boring to me. Then she'd leave the room. She always left before I could figure out what her face was saying. The light goes off in Hardly's living room and his house becomes dark. He's fallen asleep with the drunken Irishman signing to him in the background. Flora won't come home tonight and hopefully, he won't drink.

Chapter Four

I START THE fire, and the flames in the old fireplace bounce off the logs. Even though it's warm in the room, Heather shivers as she sits perched on the edge of her seat. She's on the old chair that the previous occupants left in the house when we moved in. The foam has sunk in the middle and the material showing through the seat cover is tattered from years of use. I wanted to take it to the dump but she insisted on recovering it. Her thin arms are wrapped on either side of her as though she's protecting herself. Her teeth seem to be on the verge of chattering, and she speaks quickly, barely taking a breath in between the words.

"You either believe me or you don't, Malcolm. Don't tell me something just to appease me. That doesn't work anymore. I hear it. I hear something. Do you believe in ghosts? Do you think it's a ghost?"

I try to slow her down, to calm her. I stand up and remove the screen from the front of the fireplace. Then, I take the poker and stab at the piece of wood. My dad gave it to us when we moved in. When he walked around the house he nodded, approving, and when he saw the fireplace he said that it was missing a proper poker set. So he gave us the heavy, cast-iron poker with a brush and small shovel. I carefully hang the poker on its rack. My back is to Heather but I can envision her expression before I turn. She's still barely on the edge of the chair and she looks like she's waiting for a spirit to come flying through the window any minute. There are times when she resembles the green-haired, rebellious girl whom I first met and there are other times when I wonder who she really is.

"Yes, I believe there's something out there, Heather. There are things we don't understand, but I'll tell you something. There's nothing in this house. I've checked."

She shakes her head, and quietly laughs at me.

"It's an old house. There are creaky floorboards on the floor, creaky rafters in the attic, and the pipes howl and shake. I've been over it, all of it. Nobody is here. This isn't a movie. Nobody died here. The house wasn't built on the site of an old Scottish graveyard. It's just a regular house, side by side with all the others. It's a normal neighborhood. There are no ghosts here."

She's interrupting, impatient.

"No, no, no. I know all that. That's not what I'm talking about."

I keep talking, trying to reason, trying to stop her.

"You're hearing an old house settling and getting old, that's all."

"I don't believe that. It's something else. I know it is."

"Emily doesn't hear anything. I don't hear anything. Why is that?"

She has a knowing look now. It's a new expression. In the five years we've been together I thought I'd seen everything that her face could do, but this is new. This is different.

"I'm sorry Heather, I'm sorry you're going through this."

She's still speaking quickly, but this time she whispers. Her eyes are small and burning into me. "He's here, Malcolm. He's back. You know it's him. I can almost hear him calling my name when you're over at Hardly's."

Now I understand. I close my eyes. I can't listen anymore. If Hardly hadn't started drinking again, the noises might never have happened. He'd been sober for years before Flora began her overnight excursions. He's my friend, so when he drinks I stay with him. I have to. I try to remind him of how good his life was before he went back to the bottle.

"Don't say it, Heather."

"He's been here, Malcolm. I know he has. He calls to me. I hear him in the hallway. It's not the pipes or the house, it's my father. He's here to take Emily."

It's too much to take. I stand up and pace back and forth. I'm breathing heavy, frustrated. "I watched him die, Heather. I watched John Postman die right in front of me. You know I did."

She's yelling, standing and yelling. The spit sprays from her mouth, the mouth that used to be so lovely.

"No, you saw him dying, not dead. There's a difference. We don't know what happened after we left Canada. But I'll tell you one thing. I know that beast's voice and his scent, I can smell him. He's been in this house, baiting me, calling to me, and I won't let him have her this time. This time I'll kill him myself. I will."

"Heather, remember the letters from the lawyer in Ontario who divided up his estate, remember Terry's lawyer helping us go through the process? They don't dispose of a living person's assets. Your father is dead, honey."

"I know that. I think I do." She shakes her head. I don't know if she's mocking me or trying to understand it herself. "That doesn't prove a thing. You don't know what he was like. He's evil, and I don't believe he died. He's still here."

I want to hold her, but I can't; too much has happened. Too much has changed. I'm about to throw my hands up in the air in frustration when the only voice that can save us speaks. Emily has been listening. Somehow she must have crept out of her room and she's sitting on a stair in the middle of the staircase.

"How do you know it's him?"

It shocks both of us. Heather shrinks for a moment and then we go toward our Emily. She stays on her stair, waving her hands in front of her.

"No. Leave me. Do you really think I don't know? I wasn't a baby when we came here. I was ten. I remember him. And if he's here I have a right to know, too."

I answer her immediately. "He's not here, Em. Nobody is in this house except us. I won't let anyone else in here, honey."

Heather sits down on the stair below her, reaching up, stroking her daughter's leg. The image of both of them, with their identical faces, is almost too surreal to accept, my Heather, thirty-three years old, the youthful beauty still there. Her dark, auburn hair, dyed as a teenager over and over, now its brilliant, original color hanging on her shoulders, and her green eyes, and smooth, pale skin. My Heather, whom I once loved so much. And Emily, with her mom's same piercing, luminous green eyes, and her hair pulled back behind her head in her night-time sleeping position. They're the same person, the same girl, eighteen years apart; the girls with the half-dimples on their cheeks.

Emily relaxes her body a little and folds her arms in front of herself.

"I know lots. More than you think I do."

I stand in front of them, and Heather looks up at me while she continues stroking Emily's leg. A single tear falls from her eye and she lets it glide down her cheek and drop onto her lap. It's been a long time since I saw her cry. Something stirs inside me as she speaks and I remember a little bit of who we were before we left Canada.

"Emily's right, Malcolm. We need to tell her everything. It's time we told her what happened, and why we moved here."

I knew it would come to this one day. I never thought it would be because of the threat of imaginary ghosts, but I knew one day we'd have to tell her.

"Come down here. Come sit by the fire, Em. I'll grab a blanket."

I nod to Heather and she leads our daughter into the little living room and sits her on the couch, closest to the fireplace.

"We'll tell you the story about what happened before you were born. But you need to know that everything we did was for you. We wanted you to be okay. That was the only reason."

For a while, when we got here and I reunited with my father and Hardly, it felt as though we'd found normal. It seemed as though everything was going to be okay. It felt like I'd come home and everything that had been temporary was going to become permanent. It never works like that, though. You think you've found what you're looking for, even if you don't truly know what that is, but really you haven't.

Emily looks at me with her clear eyes. "If Uncle Harry needs you to go back tonight, Malcolm, you're going to have to tell him to walk across the road and come here. You're not leaving us."

Sometimes you don't know the effect your actions have until someone makes a statement that slams you hard in your heart. "I'm not going anywhere, Emily. We'll stay here and talk."

"I know about you and mom and the lake you visited and all the lovey-dovey stuff." Her voice is dragged out in the bored fashion that only a teenage girl can have. "Tell me about me. I know some, but not all."

Heather looks stronger now; her maternal instinct is kicking in. She's sitting beside Emily and puts her arm around her while I sit on the hearth across from them.

"Okay. So you remember that I wasn't around after you were born, when you were growing up."

"Yes, Grandpa told me you moved away and didn't want to see us but I know that's not true."

Heather and I exchange looks and my strong girl is lost. She holds her daughter tighter and leaves me to take over.

"How much do you remember about him, Em?"

A tight-lipped smile She answers with a question. We're doing this her way. "Why did you come back for me when you did? Why then?"

Heather shifts a little on the couch but keeps holding on to Emily.

"Because I had to deal with the things your grandpa did to me when I was a child. When I felt I was in a better space I came back." She pauses, thinking, justifying it in her head. "I didn't want him to do the same things to you."

Silence doesn't hang in the air. That's incorrect. It surrounds you and lays heavily on everything in the room until you feel as though you're suffocating. I could see the effect on Heather and on Emily. The question that had never been asked was sitting there, waiting, but we were all afraid to ask it. Then, the one who had the most right to know spoke.

"I know already. We don't have to talk about it. I know that Grandpa abused you. I know what he did to you."

Heather's eyes acknowledge that her daughter knows. The silence comes back. I hear the flames flickering in the fireplace and I remember happier times that we spent in this room. Emily on the floor, doing her homework, asking us the answer to one of her sums, or what the capital of a country is. They're both sitting steadfast, lost. I can't do it anymore.

"Emily, do you realize exactly what your grandfather did to your mother after she became pregnant? Do you know where she was sent to?" I wait, while Emily nods, her eyes half-closed.

"I know. And I know that he took me away from her. He took your baby away."

She knows.

I pause before continuing. "You know how difficult this is then. And you know how much we love you."

"Yes, I know that." She's not defiant, just acknowledging that the suspicions she's had for years, the suspicions that form in your mind when you grow from being a child to an almost-adult, are real.

"When your grandfather took you away from your mother he threatened her. I'm not sure if you realize the type of man he was but she couldn't go back right away. But when she thought you were in danger she came to get you. We both did."

Heather whispers, as though she's talking to herself. She's looking down, staring intently at the material on the couch. "I shouldn't have waited so long. I should have gone back to get you sooner. I know that. I know that."

There is no answer but after a moment Emily leans closer into her mother.

They have the same expression on their faces. There's a resigned look in their eyes. Heather looks tired. There are little wrinkles around her mouth and she keeps her lips tight together. Emily looks the same. Then, she blinks, and there's a flicker of anger in her eyes.

"You're sure he's dead, Malcolm. My father, you're sure he died."

She said it. So now we know. We all know, and maybe she's known for a long time.

"I saw John Postman dying. He was hanging out of an overturned car on a snowy highway. His partner, the other police officer, reported to us the next day that he'd died. His affairs were settled afterward and he was buried. He deserved worse for what he did to you both, Emily, but yes, he's dead."

She stands and straightens up her body, putting her arms by her sides.

"Good, then there can be no more ghosts. Mom, nobody is here. I don't want to hear anything else about it."

It's the same tone she uses on Hardly when she tells him he can't drink anymore or when she tells him that Flora will come back to him. She'll say to him, "Uncle Harry, if you don't use your cane people are going to think you've been drinking, the way you stagger all over the place." She indulges him. She always has. She has my Scottish/Canadian accent and her mother's smile, and she hasn't been ten years old in a long time. In fact, I sometimes wonder if she ever really was. She's dismissing the situation. It's been dealt with and now we should move on.

"Mom. There are no more ghosts."

We sacrificed more for Emily than she'll ever know. All we wanted was a safe, normal life, for her, for all of us. So if it means we don't dredge up the past then we won't dredge up the past, and Heather knows that.

"There are no more ghosts, Em. They're all gone."

"Good. I'm going to bed."

She's gone through so much but she's right. Some doors should stay closed. She doesn't kiss us goodnight but when she reaches the top of the stairs she calls it back to us, leaving us with our own demons to sort out.

Chapter Five

IT TOOK ME five years of living in Scotland before I realized I needed to start running again. You reach a time in your life where you know there are certain things you need to do in order to survive. We all need to sleep, eat and drink, and I need to run. I hadn't run in years but something drew me back to it. Our schedule was simple. Heather dropped Emily off at her school and then went to her own job at the school where she worked. I'd occasionally meet clients at the house but usually the work I did was sent to me online through my computer. So I was able to schedule my own hours. I'd pull on some shorts and a T-shirt and run through the streets. I'd run down to the Dean Park and then out toward Onthank, a suburb of Kilmarnock. I'd been back running for three weeks and was beginning to get my breath back. It was still tough but I was too stubborn to stop. I've always enjoyed the long distances; I've never been able to run at any speed. The trainers call them Long Slow Distances. In training, you use them to build up your endurance. So speed was never my goal. I just wanted to get out and cover a few miles and get a sweat going, and the time after I'd try to do it a little quicker or run a little longer. The same runners seemed to run on the days when I ran. I'd nod to the less serious ones, and the ones who had their earphones attached and checked their running watches while outpacing me wouldn't even make eye contact.

She passed me almost every day. She was always on the other side of the street. Her pace was faster than mine. By the time I noticed her she was gone, and all I saw was her dark ponytail bobbing away from me above the parked cars. As my own speed increased a little and I wasn't concentrating on keeping my breath, I began to anticipate her. I'd glance on the other side of the street when I reached the area by the Dean Park where she usually passed me. On the day she spoke she actually came up from behind and said my name.

"Malcolm Wilson, look at you, still running and back in Kilmarnock." Then she laughed and before I could tell who she was, her black ponytail was beyond me and she sped off.

I told Heather about her when I got home but she was sorting out some sets of colored stars and stickers, putting them into arts and crafts kits for the children.

"Maybe she's a friend of your dad's, Malcolm. She must know you somehow. Or did you meet her at Emily's school? Is she maybe one of the other mothers?"

She doesn't look up as she asks. She keeps counting out how many stars and stickers go into each little metal box.

"I don't think that's it. She knew me from before I think."

Now she does look up, a little exasperated as she loses count.

"I'm sorry. I'll let you work."

The next day was a rest day but I ran anyway, wrenching my sore muscles. I left a little earlier than usual and strained my ears in between each of the passing cars, listening for her to come up behind me. I did not see her running that day.

The day after was my usual workout day, but I could not run fast. My calves felt heavy and strained and I had a slight pull in my Achilles. I was walking as she came up behind me and this time she did stop. I knew exactly who she was or at least I knew who she'd been. I don't remember her smiling much when we knew each other on the schoolyard and in the classroom, but when she sees me she smiles. She has the same soft brown eyes and dark hair. She no longer wears it in the old-fashioned page boy style. Now it's pulled behind her head and her slim little girl frame has developed into the rounder hips and curves of a woman. Nan McHendry had been my childhood crush. I was always too shy or scared to speak to her, so we never really became friends.

"Are you not going to say hello to me then, Malcolm? Or do you still just stare at girls?"

"I'd give you a hug, Nan, but I'm dripping with sweat."

She puts out her hand and I hold its softness.

"It's been a long time. Are you back to see your dad? Are you here on holiday?"

She falls into pace beside me and we walk together.

"I moved back here. My partner, her daughter, and myself. We came back a few years ago. We live close to where my dad is now."

"That's good. Good for your dad."

There's a different attitude toward family in the streets where I grew up. It's nothing like Canada or anywhere else I've been. Either your family will try to torture you and break you the way Hardly's parents did or they give you everything. My dad gave me everything he had and even though Nan didn't know that she was right. It was good that I was back and living close to him.

"And you Nan, which of our classmates did you end up with?"

I regret it the moment I say it. Her world may have expanded further than mine, yet I assumed she never made it out of the streets. She pauses for a moment and then begins to run. I follow her, trying to keep up.

"I'm sorry. That wasn't nice of me."

She's only a little ahead but my aching Achilles won't allow me to reach her. She turns her head slightly as she runs off. "It's okay. I wasn't always very nice to you."

As she speeds up and leaves me I call after her. "Can we run again? I'll be nicer next time."

I can't hear her. She laughs and then she may have said "yes" or maybe it was just the Scots farewell of "cheerio." I can't tell.

It's funny. You're the bullied child in school and a part of you dreams of retribution, of showing the world that mocked you that you've grown up and done something with yourself. Then, when you get the chance for redemption, you retaliate the same way they used to treat you.

I run every day for the next week, sometimes walking more than running and often hobbling. My legs feel old and heavy and my Achilles is swollen and sore. It's eight long, tired days before I see her again.

Chapter Six

THERE'S BEEN A song in my head my whole life. Well, not a song, really, more like a melody; I never can figure out the words. I've never told anybody about it, not even Malcolm, but sometimes I hear it, chirping away at me. I'll forget where I am and all of a sudden there'll be a noise as though a radio is playing far away. I pick up little pieces of the music, and I just start to figure it out and then it's gone. I never know what it is but I still recognize it. It's always the same song. I don't know if it's something I heard before I was old enough to know what music was and my mind retained it or something my head just made up. All I know for sure is that whenever I concentrate and try to figure out what the song is, the music stops.

We had five years of mostly peace and contentment in Scotland. We had the same struggles that most couples have, of course. Those perfect pairings that say they never argue and fall into each other's arms every time they lay eyes on each other don't live in the real world as far as I'm concerned, or they don't live in my real world. They can't. Life is too complicated for that and there is no consistency. I have no consistency. I have days when I wake up and I know, I absolutely know, that if I wanted to I could scrub every part of our house from top to bottom and be finished in time to prepare dinner. Or, I could recalibrate the ancient Kilmarnock Primary School filing system by the time the final bell rang. And then there are days when I don't want to get out of bed.

There are times when I feel happy. The emotion is in my mind; I can feel it and it's so vivid that I can almost touch it. And there are days when I know I'll never find it. That's just the way my mind works. It always has.

Those first few years in Scotland were easy. I never knew if I was really going to stay and that made it feel like a long vacation. In Canada, when I ran away from my father and everything that happened, the days varied between wanting to be a good, conservative member of society and wanting to tear my skin off because I couldn't stand myself. But that's not me anymore. Coming to Kilmarnock meant that my years of running from my past back home in Canada were behind me. I still have the memories of what happened to me as a little girl, they don't go away, but I've tried to leave them back there. I won't allow them to control me.

Emily was the missing piece of my life, and Malcolm helped me find her. He didn't come to my rescue, and he wasn't my hero. He just made me feel capable. He touched something inside me that made me go back for her. I would always have gone back but he made me want to do it sooner. I used to think it was because I wanted him and me to have a fresh start with no secrets but I'm not sure about that anymore. I think I saw something in him when he told me about his childhood and it touched a basic, gut instinct in me. I knew I'd failed. I failed to go back for her and I failed to protect her.

We'd known each other for about ten minutes before going to Ontario to find Emily. I lied to him because the truth was too despicable to share. I told him it was someone else but I knew he'd figure it out by himself eventually anyway. And he gave me a happy ending for a little while. There was so much promise in those early days and sometimes it felt like enough. There are just never enough of those days.

When I have my darker times, I try to remind myself that although Malcolm helped me find Emily, he didn't save me. I saved me. I went back and confronted the man who took my childhood from me. Malcolm helped and I couldn't have done it without him but I need to believe that I saved myself because if I don't I can't be me, I can't be Heather. Malcolm has always told me that. At first, when we moved back here, he'd say, "We did it together. We saved Emily but you confronted him, you went back and dug it up so that you could claim your daughter."

Then, when he'd see that I was down on myself or having a day where I couldn't function, he'd change it, and say, "You did it, Heather. None of this happens without your courage. Don't forget that. Without you having the strength to face your father, we don't have a family."

I know what he's doing and I appreciate it, and there are times when I believe him. I adjust the story in my head because it feels like we do have a family and I value that. I remember the talk we had at the lake at the end of the world, I remember what Malcolm went through in that town when we found my father, but I also remember that I was there, too, and he's right. I saved Emily and when I did I saved myself, too. And then, just when my head begins to calm and I believe that the memory of my father will leave me alone and I start to forget what happened, he comes back. His stinking, reeking presence comes back to torture me.

He came to our house again a few nights ago when Malcolm was at Hardly's. If it's not him then he's sent his dirty, evil spirit to haunt me. Sometimes I agree with Malcolm and Emily and I believe he is dead but other times I'm convinced he's here, watching us. I'm careful. When I'm at work I watch for movement from the windows of the classroom and sometimes I double back when I'm out walking to the shops in case he's stalking me. I've never seen him but I can feel his presence, I know he's here. Malcolm may be convinced that he died but I am not.

I heard his voice one day. I was in the classroom setting up for the fourth year students. The work is simple. I'm the most over-qualified teacher's assistant in the history of teacher's assistants. I could do more, find something else, but something's holding me back, stopping me from fulfilling my potential. I just haven't figured out what it is yet.

These kids are easy. I arrange the desks, clean the blackboards and wait for the teacher. It's normal. Everything is the same way it always is. There's the usual yelling and calling in the hallways from the children and from somewhere in the midst of it all I hear his voice call my name. It's within the voices of the children. Their nattering continues; they're oblivious to it. They don't hear him. But I do, and once again I fail. I drop to my knees and crawl to a desk and push it in front of me keeping it between me and the door. Then I wait for him. Gilly Brown comes in before the children. For once she's early and she knows right away that something is wrong. She turns back and calls outside to have the children line up in the hallway instead of coming in right away. Then she comes to me and puts her hands on my shoulders.

She doesn't ask what's wrong. I'm the strange woman from Canada who helps at the school that her daughter doesn't attend anymore. "Heather, I need to get the children in here. Why don't you go and see the headmaster."

I straighten myself up and wipe my eyes with the back of my hand. When I look back at her, she's still watching me but her mind is on the children in the hallway. I suppose you can only handle so much drama at one time and she's probably had her fill for the day. "Go on love, go to the office and have a wee break."

The children don't notice. They're too busy pushing each other. The little boys pretending they don't like the little girls and the little girls participating in the popularity contest that we all put ourselves through. I look up and down the hallway and all the classroom doors are closed. No one's here; he's gone.

I just want to go home. I'm going to grab my jacket from the staff room, which the teachers reluctantly allow me access to, and make my way home, but when I look back at Mrs. Brown's door she's still standing there herding the last of the children inside. With her free hand, she waves me toward the office. Her smile tells me that I'll feel better if I go there. I have no choice.

The headmaster is out but his assistant is in. I'd met Barry before but I'd never been sent to the office. That's what I tell him. He begins to laugh but when I don't laugh back he takes me inside and tells me to sit down while he makes us a cup of tea. The Scots and their medicinal tea. We laughed about that, but that was later; we saved that for another day. I can't tell him about hearing my father's voice; I can't put it into words. Instead, I tell him about the song that plays inside my head. And he's very helpful. He knows what I'm talking about. He knows what is wrong with me and he knows what I have to do to fix it. He says he'll help me. That was how it began.

Chapter Seven

MY DAD BEGAN giving his money away. He didn't have much. He has a small pension from the government and one from the brief national service when he served his country as a young man. And I suppose he probably had some savings, too. He paid rent on his home for many years and when the council gave him a deal on purchasing his house he managed, with the help of a loan from the bank, to do it, but that was paid off long ago. He never seemed to lack the basics that he required. His fridge and cupboards were usually full of the foods that he liked. He doesn't drive anymore, deciding to use public transit, so he didn't have a car to throw money at, and he even attended an occasional football match now and again. Then things began to change.

He had the telephone company change his phone number, twice in eight months. He walked down to our house one day, holding a slip of paper. He'd written his full name in block letters and he had his new phone number underlined. He said he was getting too many harassing phone calls. My father has always been a large, strong man. His wisdom is simple. If a man says he's going to do something he does it. You should be paid fairly for an honest day's work. And if someone needs a hand you step up and help out. I wait a day and then drop by his house to ask him about the changing numbers. As we sit in his kitchen while he opens a can of soup, I notice my breath puffing in front of me as I speak.

"Dad, what's your heat set to?"

The man I grew up with would have given me a straight answer but as my dad has gotten older he evades questions from time to time. Part of the reason is his diminished hearing but I think part of it is also the fact that he wants some time to process before answering.

"The heat? You need heat?"

"Yes, Dad, it's freezing in here. I can see my breath."

That's when I realize he has his jacket on while he stands in front of the stove stirring the soup.

"I don't have it on. I like it fresh. Put your coat back on if you're cold."

I get up and turn the thermostat up and wait for the blower to kick in.

"Malcolm, just leave it. Now do you want your soup or are you going home?" He bangs the spoon on the side of the pot as he questions me.

I decide to ignore it for now. I turn the heat back down. My father doesn't often get angry so I eat soup with him and stay quiet, in the cold, deciding not to ask any more about his heat or why he's changed his phone number yet again.

The phone calls somehow reach us at home. I'm not sure how, perhaps they found another Wilson who lives in the vicinity and they took a chance. Heather answers the first one and with a confused expression she hands the phone to me. It's someone in Nigeria, or so they claim. In broken English they ask for my father by his full name and when I tell them I'm his son, they ask if there's a way to reach him as they've been trying for several days. When I ask who they are and what their business with my dad is they tell me that they aren't at liberty to say. I don't often lose my temper but it's my dad. As I press the man he hangs up the phone.

When I call his new phone number, the phone just rings and rings. It's Wednesday evening, so I know he's home. I pull on my shorts and t-shirt and jog around to his house in the uncharacteristically warm Kilmarnock night. His living room light is on and when he sees me he opens the door with a big grin on his face.

"You're running again. Good. That's good, son."

"Dad, you're not answering your phone. I've been calling."

There's no change in his expression. "Too many nutcases call at night. I just let it ring. I might have the number changed again; I'm still getting lots of wrong numbers."

It's frustrating, but I don't know what to say. So, again, I let it go.

On days when our schedules allow us to visit him, especially when we all arrive on his doorstep at the same time, he's calm and happy. He acts like a man who has been waiting, and I suppose to some extent he has been. He's been waiting for something his whole life and it finally arrived. He had a lady friend at one time and they seemed close. Joy had her own home and they'd visit occasionally, but after a few months, she moved away, deciding to move in with her daughter in England. Plans were made for shared holidays and visits but unfortunately none of them materialized. He wasn't heartbroken, though. He accepted that this was what the world was offering him. And I believe he enjoyed spending the time he gained with Hardly and Flora and Heather and me, and especially Emily, more than the time he'd been spending with his lady friend.

He dines with us once a week and on one other night during the week I go over and watch the fitba on television with him, cheering in his living room for our team, Glasgow Celtic. He was always tidy and organized but when his girlfriend moved away his house became cluttered. He seemed to care less about putting things in their proper places. When he goes to the bathroom during the half time break I look at the piles of books sitting on his dining room table. There are books on self-help and books on hypnosis, and books on how to get rich quick, lots of books on how to increase your wealth. There are stacks of mail amongst the books, some letters are open and some are still in their envelopes. They're from all over the world and the printing on the outsides claims that inside there are unclaimed funds. People from Australia, India, and Germany all want to send my dad money. I put a few of the unopened letters as well as one from the bottom of the pile that had been opened into my pockets and plop myself back onto my chair before he returns to the living room.

"You know, Dad, Heather thinks we have ghosts in the house. She hears noises. She's sure something is there. She hears them when I'm across the street with Hardly."

I wait and expect him to show his typical sensible side and explain that all the old houses in the neighborhood have creaks and groans. But he doesn't.

"Ghosts? I wouldn't be surprised. There's a book I can lend her. It'll explain what type of spirit is inhabiting your house."

He starts searching through books in his bookshelf. There's an old framed black and white picture of a man wearing some type of turban and a polar neck sweater that he moves out of the way.

"Who's that in the picture, Dad?"

He holds it and looks over at me as he finds the book.

"Aha. That's who I'm looking for. Tell her to read this. He's extremely well-respected in the continent. I picked this up at the second-hand bookstore."

He hands me a book that has the same picture of the man on the cover. The paperback is old and yellowed and the title claims to teach the reader how to commune with the spirits in order to benefit financially from their wisdom.

It takes every bit of strength within me to not mock him. I need to know more but it's very difficult to not at least question it.

"What continent Dad? I don't understand."

He looks at me as though we've spoken about this very thing many times. All of a sudden I feel as though I'm the one who is wrong.

"I don't know what continent. *The* continent. Read it for yourself. This man knows what he's talking about."

The game is back on and he clicks the remote control to un-mute the television as the players take the field. I watch him from the corner of my eye. His eyes seem more sunken back into his head than they ever have before. The age is there but there's more. There's also a confused look that I don't remember seeing before.

When I get home I open the letters. They're junk mail but they're written as though he's been corresponding with them already. The form letters have a tear-off section where you can enter your credit card number or bank account information and the company will automatically debit funds from your account. And in return, you'll earn untold wealth. It will come to you. In fact, in one you have to specify whether you'd like to receive ten million pounds in a lump sum or in monthly increments. The letter that's been opened has the same type of fill-out section and my dad has already filled in most of it. It's the same type of gibberish and he's ticked off that he'd like to receive his money all at once. There's also a section where he must attest that when he receives the power, that I assume will allow him to come into contact with the money, that he will use it only for positive purposes. He must never share the power with anyone other than to help another human being in a positive manner. He's ticked all of the boxes.

My father didn't fill out that form. It was his writing but the man who raised me and preached common sense wouldn't have filled that nonsense out. If he'd received this while I was living at home when I was growing up, he would have sent them away on the horse they rode in on. He had little patience for fools. The only excuses he made were for me and then later for Hardly, too. He even excused my mother for leaving him and moving back to Canada. He was an intelligent man and a patient soul. I knew he wasn't rich, but I don't know why he's filling out forms that are so obviously scams and trying to fall into buckets of money. It seems like age is taking something from him and he's searching for a replacement.

I start picking mail out of his mailbox before the letters reach him. They are more of the same type of junk – promising that millions of pounds will come into his life if he sends a donation to a Kenyan doctor who will bless him in a return letter. Or, he'll become the benefactor of an American industrial magnate who will send him part of his fortune. I can tell from the correspondence that he's replied to many of them. He's sent money orders giving away his meager savings to whichever confidence game is targeting him. And once he's on their books the bastards are relentless, never leaving him alone.

I wait until we're working in his yard. He's talked about growing tomatoes for years so I bought him a mini-greenhouse. It's a small kit that you install along the edge of your house and put stakes into the ground, then sheet it in with plastic. Basically, you're growing tomatoes along the side of your house and the plastic keeps them from getting too cold in the unpredictable Scottish summers. We hold the plastic in our hands and stretch it along the wall. He's attaching a stake at his end while I'm doing mine.

"Keep it straight, Malcolm. They grow straight up, son, remember?" He winks and I smile back. There's still a lot of power in his hands as he easily pushes the stakes into the dirt.

"Dad."

"Malcolm."

He's having a happy day. He's happy that I'm home, that we're all here. I can see that. He smiles his crinkly smile as he gently mocks me.

"Dad, what's with all the get rich quick books and the junk mail? What's going on with all that stuff?"

An uncharacteristic pause. Again, this isn't like my dad. He waits before answering.

"Just stuff I'm reading. Some of it is very interesting information and it's not readily available to the ordinary man on the street."

"It kind of looked like junk mail to me Dad. What type of information are you getting from it?"

The sheeting is tight on the stakes and we're standing looking at what we've done. Now he's frustrated with me. This is a new look for him.

"How do you know it's junk, Malcolm? How do you know? There might be something to it."

"Okay, Dad, you might be right." I push the other stake into my side and he immediately does the same.

I don't want to talk about any money that he might have sent to them. So I leave it. He knows I'm watching him now though and I'll have to be more careful.

When I walk across the street to see Hardly, Flora is moving quickly around the living room picking up sections of a newspaper. She looks agitated as though they've been fighting again. She's here, though and Hardly seems sober. When I ask them if I should come back, Flora insists that I stay.

"It's Dad. I thought the two of you should know what's happening to him."

They know already. They've noticed it, too. Flora has had some experience. "My Gran went the same way, Malcolm. He's going to be okay, just keep your eye on him. We all will."

She looks over at Hardly, and opens her eyes wide, prodding him. He waits a moment and muses, looking down as though he doesn't want to admit it out loud. "He talks to me about his experience during the war, Malcolm, about all the things he did as a soldier. He tells me stories about his military career and then he'll stop suddenly and move onto something else."

"Military career? My dad wasn't in a war. He did his military service but that was short and uneventful. I remember him talking about it a long time ago."

Flora is nodding but it's Hardly who answers. "I know that. He makes it up. It's just where his brain goes, and then he straightens himself out again."

Flora is sitting on the edge of the couch, watching me. They've talked about this. Maybe they didn't want to tell me, they weren't sure how I'd react. "He's going to be okay, it's just what happens to some people as they get older."

"He's not old yet. This shouldn't be happening at his age."

Hardly is about to agree with me when Flora cuts in. She looks at both of us as she speaks. "It is, though and we'll deal with it." She's practical and caring at the same time. She might have spent time in Ireland but her sensibility is Scottish.

"I'm thinking we should take turns dropping in to see him. If we do it every day maybe he'll tell me what's happening."

Flora shakes her head. "We can do that, but you can't let him lose his independence. You know your dad."

She's right but I can't just sit back and wait for it to get worse. Over the next few days I make excuses to drop by his house. Sometimes I take Hardly and Emily with me. He's always pleased to see Hardly and gives him a hug that's reserved just for him, and of course, when he sees Emily his eyes have a special light in them.

My dad begins by asking after Flora. "And where is your Scottish, Irish girl tonight, son? You should be with her instead of here bothering with me."

Hardly seems as though he's embarrassed to answer. "She's packing, getting ready to head back up north. There's another family crisis she has to deal with."

He put his hand on Hardly's shoulder. "Absence makes the heart grow fonder. You'll be fine."

Then he rests his gaze on Emily.

"And where is that busy mother of yours? Sorting out that high school so that they know who they're dealing with when you start going there? Or, keeping your house in order? Tell her she needs to visit sometimes."

"No, Grandpa, she's at the primary school. I'm at the high school now. She stayed when I moved on."

"Well, remind her of my address, please. I can write it down for you if you like."

Emily giggles and puts her arms around his waist. She's too old for him to swoop up anymore. His actions aren't as swift as they once were but I still think of him as an able, strong man.

We sit and visit and after a few minutes, he again asks after Heather. Emily and I have become used to it and we answer just as politely as we did the first time. After two weeks of random visits, he takes me aside. Heather has accompanied me this time and after saying good night to him she stands at his front gate looking into the street as two young boys pass by.

"I'm fine Malcolm. The daily check-ups are very kind but I'm doing fine."

"I'm just worried, Dad. You don't seem yourself these days with new phone numbers and no heat in the house. It's a bit worrisome."

There's another pause. The pauses that were never there before are more frequent now. The man who would answer instinctively is gone. Now it's a measured, mysterious response that I get. He gives me a little wink as he answers. "Everything is fine, son. And soon things are going to be even better, for all of us."

He puts his arm around me and squeezes my shoulder and before I have a chance to examine his face or even ask another question he calls "Cheerio" to Heather and closes the door behind himself.

Chapter Eight

THERE ARE ABSOLUTELY no coincidences in life. None. Everything happens for a reason. I'm sure of it. I don't mean the coincidences that you see on predictable television programs or read in cheap books. Those are contrived. The real life coincidences happen for a reason. The fact that Nan and I were both runners was a coincidence, but I was due to bump into her at some point. It never happened at the corner store or in town. It happened when we were running. There are only so many areas in my neighborhood where you can run, and most of us migrate to the park. We don't always want to run through the Dean Park although from time to time that was the route we chose to take, but we do want to be close to it. We crave the life and energy that emits from the trees and we want the green, even if it comes from the football field down below. We need it to interrupt the greyness of the houses with their postage stamp sized yards and their identical doors and windows.

"I waited here to see the Queen one year. I was with my mother. It was before she moved back to Canada."

Nan is slightly ahead of me and looks back to answer. "Oh, I remember that. She used to come every year. The whole town took a day off to see the wave. She'd slow down, her big car cruising past and she'd wave out the window before she went back to London to her palace. I always wanted her to stand up so I could see what she was wearing. She never did, though."

Nan stops suddenly and moves her hand slowly, imitating her royal majesty's wave.

"What was up with that anyway? Why did she come to Kilmarnock?"

We're at the park entrance. This is where we decide whether we're going to run down the hill and up the other side to the Burns monument or keep on the street and make our way back to our neighborhoods. It's not a steep hill but we've already run a few miles and my legs are feeling heavy. She looks at me pleadingly and I reluctantly accept her challenge and follow her down the footpath, running behind her while she answers me.

"I don't really know. Maybe she ran out of places to wave and we were all she had left. This is a small country after all, Malcolm. This isn't Canada."

I keep my eyes upright as I follow her, politely not focusing on her rear end as she winds her way over the bridge and down the trail toward the football field. When we reach it, she's a few feet in front of me and some of the boys playing below call out, admiring her form. She's used to it and ignores them.

"Is your mom still over there? Do you hear from her?"

"I do."

She looks back and smiles, then slows down a little, letting me catch my breath. She doesn't stop, though. She keeps running, not letting me off the hook.

"I phone her when I think about it. She's always on the go somewhere, another man, another romance. She's never happy. Always on the move to someplace different."

She keeps looking forward and doesn't answer. Maybe there isn't an answer. My mother and I have a strange relationship. We always have. I don't think she ever wanted to be a mother. She wanted to bask in the accolades when I outperformed my classmates or ran a long distance race. Then she'd remind anyone who would listen that she'd had a hand in raising me. But when it came to teaching me the basics, she never wanted to participate. I had my father for that, though. He was always there to show me where the line in the sand was.

She's striding effortlessly up the incline toward the Burns monument. She slows a little, making sure I'm still behind her. When we reach the top, I stop. I have no choice; I have no breath left. We run ten and ones, ten minutes running and then a one minute walk break. We're not due a break but she always gives me a short reprieve at the top of the hill. She stretches her thigh, pushing her foot against the base of the statue and I look over the playing fields where the boys are playing football or fitba as we locals call it. I look over to where the road leads to the cemetery and finally I turn back and look up at the imposing statue of Robert Burns, the Scots poet who grew up a few miles from Kilmarnock. Around the statue, there are a few empty beer cans that have been tossed aside recklessly and a bag with the name of a fast food chain on it. There's graffiti with the name of a local boy's gang sprayed onto a wall to the side but the statue is amazingly intact.

"They never damage the statue. It looks the same as it did when we were kids. I wonder why? I remember Hardly and I climbed up to the top of it once. It felt kind of strange once we were up there standing beside Rabbie, so we got down again right away."

She straightens up after stretching out her calves and puts her hands on her hips and smiles at me. She's twelve and twenty and forty all at the same time. She has the same expression that will attract men to her until the day she dies. Her perfectly straight teeth, thin, red lips and the mischievous twinkle in her eyes. "Exactly, it's a Scots thing. We're proud of our history and we love Burns. Doesn't matter if you're the blue-haired menace with the safety pins through your forehead, you respect it. It's Rabbie Burns; you don't mess with Burns."

I smile back at her and she tempts me.

"Cemetery?"

"Shit. Really?"

She's laughing and is off before I can talk her out of it as we extend our distance and head toward the cemetery. She pauses at the main road. I catch her and we wait for a gap between the passing cars.

"I remember you and Hardly climbing things. My goodness, that was a long time ago. Terrible things we did to each other as children, Malcolm. I suppose they're not much better to each other now."

When I finally found her again after my initial verbal flub, we took to just running and enjoying general talk about the town. I'd tell her about Canada from time to time but she never mentioned a family or a relationship. She wears a gold band indicating she's married but she's never spoken of anyone.

"You asked me when we first ran into each other who I ended up with."

"I was being an ass. I shouldn't have assumed that you never left here."

We run across the street, falling into stride beside each other. The consistency of our pace makes it feel as though we're helping each other along the pavement.

"I married Stuart Douglas."

I haven't thought of his name in years. For a time, early in my life, the boy who tormented Hardly and I was almost continuously in my thoughts. I'd waken to think of what he was going to do to me that day and I'd go to bed plotting his revenge. It's difficult to know what to say so I say nothing.

"He was good to me, Malcolm. He was the best of the bunch and you know university was never really an option. I couldn't be away from my mam. She had her health issues so I stayed. I married Stuart and for a while, it was all very good. Then everything went to shite."

We're at the entrance to New Farm Loch, the housing development built in the seventies. It looks the same as it always did. White houses built to look more modern than the row homes that I grew up in. She swerves us off on a street. This is her town and I know the route will eventually take us back to our neighborhood.

I think the worst and ask, expecting it. "What happened?"

"He died Malcolm. Cancer, three years ago. Then my mam last year."

It doesn't matter who it is or what they did to us. At our age, it doesn't make sense. "I'm sorry. That's far too young to go. I'm really sorry."

We run along the pavement and then jump off the curb and onto the road to avoid a woman pulling a cart. When we're past her, she blows her nose into her handkerchief and it makes a long, bellowing sound. We hold our laughter until we're well past the woman and then together we break the tension and let it out.

"I thought it was the old rag and bones man when I heard that. Man, that was some sound."

"Rag and bones man? The man that used to collect all the old dishes and linens from the houses? Malcolm, you have been away for a long time."

And then we're back. Somehow her route has looped us around and we're at the intersection where she leaves me as she heads home to her house and I run to mine.

"Yes, it's been a very long time."

She doesn't look sad but it's difficult not to ask. I have to.

"Are you okay?"

Smiling, she indulges me as though she's still the popular girl on the playground and I'm the awkward kid who stares too much.

"I'm sound. I'm fine. Life happens. You take your comforts where you can, and you never, ever have any regrets. Never."

As she runs off, I call after her. "Tomorrow, or next day?"

"Tomorrow if you like. I'll be at our usual place."

I walk toward my house, straightening out my leg and stretching the muscles, smiling. We have a usual place.

Chapter Nine

WE CALL EACH other once a week through our computers. He installed a program from all the way across the world and he's able to access my computer from his. I'll wake up and the pop-up menu on my screen will have unfamiliar programs listed. He's been able to do these types of things since he was a young boy. It's 2002 and the changes he told me about years ago are becoming real now. He's always been ahead of everyone else.

I type in my password. It rings up his computer and his face pops up on my screen and mine on his. I have no idea how he does it and when I tell people they don't believe me, but then again they don't know Terry. He went from building a homemade car wash in the back lot of his father's automotive dealership to designing electronic toys for children and adults, and then he left it all behind. He tells me that now he just deals with money, nothing else. He says that money has no emotions like people. Money is just money, that's all. I know a little bit about money; I've been an accountant my whole working life, but when Terry starts talking about money, he talks about it as though it is a real, living entity, not just a commodity and it sounds like it does indeed have emotions. He talks about leveraging and building and hedging and even defaulting. He deals with banks and currencies and sometimes countries, too. You'll never hear about Terry McAllister in the news or even see his name on the letterhead of one of his companies but his funds are behind lots of things that happen in the world.

He leaned into his computer screen once, the way he used to lean toward me when he'd take me into his confidence, and told me something interesting. He said that he doesn't trade in dollar or pound or yen amounts. His currency is information. Information is what earns revenue. Information is what interests him. So when I couldn't find any information on John Postman's death or even his history through libraries and long distance phone calls to government agencies, I knew he'd be able to help me.

As the screen lights up, I can see him as though he's sitting right across from me, his proud smile beaming across the miles.

"How's the picture, Malcolm? I remotely updated your camera. You should be able to see the whiteness of my teeth shining back at you."

Jo, his wife, leans over his shoulder before I can answer and he gives her a friendly grimace as she steals his thunder for a moment.

"Say something, Malcolm. Let me here it, please."

"It's been a grand day ower here, Jo."

She feigns anger at me and leans further over Terry's shoulder. "No, your real voice, quit messing around. I want to hear if it's gotten any stronger."

"It's nice to see you, too, Jo. You're looking exceptionally lovely today and yes, Terry, the picture is clearer this time. I can see a couple of lines around your eyes, though. I've never noticed them before."

"Your accent gets stronger each time we talk to you, Scottish boy. Man, did you ever live here at all? Love you and love to Heather and Emily and your dad, too." She blows a kiss as she walks away from the computer. I hear her voice from somewhere behind Terry, still talking about me. "Oh, and Terry, make sure you tell Malcolm about his mother."

Terry shakes his head at me and points his finger at the screen. "I have no lines on my face; stop kidding around. Now, I got your email and I must say I uncovered a couple of interesting things. Did you know that the Postmans, Heather's family, pretty well built that town? And, there are still some parcels of land there registered in the family name."

The fact that Jo knows something about my mother is confusing me. He sees it in my face and puts his hands up before answering. "Okay, here's the thread, stay with me. Are you ready?"

I don't know if I am but I tell him to go ahead anyway.

"Jo volunteers at the hospital; it's hospice work, sitting with people who have no family. While she was there she encountered a band of gypsies…"

"There's no such thing as gypsies anymore."

He laughs, "No, believe me, there is. A band of gypsies or a group of rough looking characters who sleep outside and probably slaughter chickens and pilfer from little old ladies are trying to check one of their own into the emergency ward. None of them have a medical card or even identification."

"Gypsies, really?" I'm dreading how my mother might be involved.

Jo's been listening to us. Her voice calls from somewhere behind Terry. "Guys, don't use that word. Those folks were Romani people; don't use the other word."

"Sorry honey, Romani people. And yes, Malcolm, really. Keep listening. There's a woman with them and she offers her medical card to use as payment for one of the Romani men. It isn't going to work of course but the group of them is trying to figure out a way to scam the hospital using this woman's identity. Jo is passing in the hallway and overhears the gist of the conversation. Well, something makes her turn. The woman was your mom, Malcolm. Jo's seen photos of her and then she heard one of the men read her name from her medical card."

It's beginning to make sense. Almost.

55

"So Jo, being the benevolent Florence Nightingale that she is," he turns his head backward looking for his wife, "introduces herself and pays for the fellow to have some stitches put into his arm. He was cut with a bottle apparently, but not from fighting or drinking. He made that perfectly clear."

"My mom's with a gypsy. I mean, a Romani person."

"Yes, and Jo found out that they're traveling some kind of a circuit through the Interior of British Columbia all summer – Kelowna, Vernon, Penticton. Shouldn't be hard to find them to see what she's up to."

There's an unopened letter from my mother sitting on my kitchen counter. I've ignored it but now I can't wait to read what it says.

"Okay, you can thank Jo and her sleuthing skills for that morsel of information. Now let me tell you about this land."

"I don't care Terry. I just need confirmation that the old man died. John Andrew Postman, why can't I find his obituary? Do the cops keep that stuff classified? He was just a regular country police captain."

He doesn't hear me. He's talking into the air, not looking at the screen, and the microphone doesn't seem to be working on my side again. He keeps talking about land and deeds and titles, things that he'd be interested in but not me. He doesn't know what happened five years ago, not everything. If he did he'd realize that I just need confirmation that the man is dead.

"It's held in some kind of a family trust and here's the really interesting part – there's been some movement lately because of the pipeline. A couple of parcels have been put up for sale. I'm having Tyler, the young appraiser I told you about, look into it further for us. Quite honestly it might be worth taking a look at. Heather should be interested in this; those assets should belong to her."

I know Heather relinquished her interests in her father's estate, and gave it all up to a distant uncle that she'd never met. Terry's lawyer helped us with that, but I thought it only consisted of the home he'd been living in. I need to get Terry back on track. I type into the little text box that accompanies the program and tell him that he can't hear me and I ask him again what I want to know, but he keeps talking into the air as though he's addressing a room full of people.

"Oh, you probably don't know what's happening in Northern Ontario but there's been another natural gas discovery. None of the land in the Postman parcels are part of the area that has minerals but it's close, really damn close. So chances are they're trying to interest a development company and that's why…"

His eyes drop to where he can see what I typed on the screen and when he looks up his face has changed. He's gone from excited businessman to something a little more fragile.

"That's what I'm trying to tell you, Malcolm. I can't confirm that John Postman is dead. Somebody listed several parcels of the land for sale. If it's not him then it has to be somebody acting on his behalf." He pauses. His eyes flicker for a moment before he continues. Maybe he does know. Everything happened so fast back then and I don't remember what I told him.

"Malcolm, there is a possibility that her father is still alive."

Chapter Ten

GOING TO SCHOOL helped Emily adjust and it helped her decipher the different accents but it took me a long time to hear the difference in all of their dialects. Early on, I referred to a man who was calling out on the street one day as having an unusual Scottish accent only to have Malcolm and his dad immediately chime back in unison, "He's English."

I'd never known either of them to be exclusionary but when it came to English people, the rules seemed to change. They yelled it as though the man had no business walking down one of their revered Scottish sidewalks. From then on, I gave up trying to figure out where people were from. I made an exception with Flora, though. She's been my angel. She has a lovely Irish lilt in her voice that shines through her Scots accent every so often. She and I both came here from the outside. She doesn't understand my problem, the problem I have in my head, but she has empathy, and sometimes her purring voice makes me feel better. She grew up in Scotland but then lived in Ireland for a while. So I have Flora when she's here and not running around with girlfriends I don't know or straightening out family business in northern Scotland. She's been good to Emily, too. Emily loves her Auntie Flora and of course she has a special relationship with her Uncle Harry. With Hardly, Emily was always the adult, right from the beginning. When she was a little girl, I'd watch her from our front window when she crossed the quiet street to go from our house to theirs. Flora would phone me just as she was crossing back and I'd wait for her. We had a usual routine that we'd go through.

I stand with my hands on my hips. "Well, how are Aunt Flora and Uncle Harry today?"

"He's limping again. He says it only happens when it rains but he's fibbing. Again."

I brush the palm of my hand on her little back as she walks past me through our front door. I know the game he plays with her and so does she. He'll wink at Emily and she'll shake her head and grip his arm, helping him support his weight as they walk around their little house. Apparently, he's limped since he lost part of his leg after serving in Ireland, but recently it's been worse, more pronounced. Emily indulges him. She always has.

As she grew older she developed her own personality and her own unique accent, too. She actually sounds a bit like Malcolm. Some days I see some of myself in her while other days I'm not sure who she is.

She has two close friends and they adore her. Sometimes, I find myself jealous of the relationship the three of them have with each other. They talk about boys, but Em seems more focused on her schooling than relationships. And they talk about music. One of her friends has a ring in her nose and a tattoo of the Scots thistle on her forearm. She's a delightful girl and her unique marks of rebellion are a contrast to her soft voice and polite manners. Her name is Fiona and when she speaks, she stares with intense blue eyes that disarm you if you look into them for too long. And Emily's best friend is Lorraine. Lorraine is loud, much louder than the other two and I wonder how she became part of the little circle. The dynamics between the three are interesting. I have time to watch them. We get home from school about the same time and Malcolm will be working in his office or spending time with his dad or out running again. Either Fiona or Lorraine could be the ringleader; both have the personalities that could carry it off. They're not, though. They defer to Emily. She's the sensible one. She has a serious, almost maternal side that neither of them understands and it sets her apart. I don't think she's shared her childhood story with her friends, or at least not the whole story. Maybe they take her solemnness as wisdom or perhaps they just enjoy being around her. I'm not sure. The night she asked to go to see a band with her friends was the first night we all laughed together at the same time in a long while.

Malcolm asked the question that seemed to matter most to him, but I couldn't understand why. "What are they called, Emily? This band that the three of you have to absolutely go and see?"

Fiona answers quickly and then Emily stares her into silence. "Naked Pictures of my Mother."

With zero hesitation Malcolm answers. "So, that would be a no from me. A great, big, fat no actually, ladies."

They glare back at him. I know what it's like to rebel, and I've heard the older kids at my primary school talk about the band. "I know them. They're local aren't they?"

Emily sees an opening and thinks she might win. "Yes, Mom, they're from Kilmarnock. From Killie. Fiona's brother will be there and tons of other people we know."

Lorraine and Fiona make whining noises and as usual Lorraine's voice drowns out Fiona's as she turns to Malcolm. In the old days he'd be Mr. Wilson but kids these days are different, even in Scotland. "Yes, Malcolm, we'll be supporting local talent."

Fiona, with her serious, softer voice chimes in, looking at both of us. "And we'd be very, very good girls. We'd have Emily home as early as possible."

Malcolm and his twisted reasoning is still stuck on the name of the band. "Naked Pictures Of My Mother? Whatever happened to the Bay City Rollers? They played here in Kilmarnock once you know. Or what about Springsteen and the E Street Band? That man changed my life."

Emily keeps pushing. "Well, maybe Naked Pictures will change mine, Dad."

She's looking at Malcolm for permission. It's strange but she seems to think it should be up to him. He looks at me. His mouth is half open and for just a moment he looks like the beautiful boy I first fell in love with. A little bit of me wants to cry, he's so lovely.

I whisper to him, loud enough for all of them to hear. "Let her go."

Over the din of them celebrating, he tries to make himself heard. "I'm dropping you off and picking you up and if you're not where we agree to meet, I'll *come in, jump up on the stage and have the lead singer of Naked Pictures"* he shakes his head, slowly, deliberately trying to make his point, *"announce that your father is here to pick you up."*

When it's over, we laugh. They're happy and I'm happy. She's expressing herself and finding out what she likes and this is good, but it feels like something else just happened. I feel like I lost a little bit of her tonight. Not just to adulthood and its complexities but to Malcolm, too. I don't understand it but I feel it. I know it's there.

Chapter Eleven

KILMARNOCK GIVES US an uncommonly warm morning. I sit in my office on the second floor of our house and watch a young girl twirling in circles as she walks down the pavement. The cracked light from the sun is sneaking through the clouds as she dances around last night's rain puddles. Something is making her giggle. Maybe it's the rare heat from the sun, or maybe it's the freedom of being a child. I don't know. I sit up straight and hope that somewhere there's a mother or father watching her as she dances. I'm right; a moment later a man calls to her, not chiding her, just watching and being there. She's nine or ten, about the same age Emily was when we moved here, and the same age I was when my mother took me away from my father and moved us to Canada.

I remember some of it but not all of it. I don't remember them fighting. I don't think that was the cause. My father never raised his voice when I was a child. My mother did though, and somehow he always managed to appease her. I suppose when he stopped being able to do that, she moved on, and she took me with her. There are lots of things I don't remember. I don't remember saying goodbye to him. Maybe he couldn't do it and thought it would be easier to just let us go. He would have done what was best for me. That's the kind of man my father has always been. I remember the airplane flight, though. I remember it because I was a secret agent in those days. I was the type of agent who could scare off another man with a squint of my eyes or a menacing tilt of my chin. In my mind I had the physical toughness, too. I was somewhere between James Bond and Bruce Lee, the guy from the movie, *Enter the Dragon*. I hadn't seen the film but I'd overheard a neighbor telling my dad about it. Bruce Lee was tough and mysterious, and the James Bond comparison was obvious. I was Scottish so like most little boys I tried to emulate Scotland's Bond, Sean Connery.

So, there I sat, the squinting secret agent on a plane bound for Canada from Prestwick airport while the nice Canadian stewardess asked me if I had something bothering my eye. She didn't realize that I was looking around to see if there were any other secret agents on the flight that I might give a discreet nod to.

My new pants had been purchased for the flight and the flight only, so I'd never worn them before. They were itchy and it was hot on the plane. It was a different type of hot from anything I'd experienced before. It was making me sweat not just on my forehead but in my armpits, too, and the little cup of ginger ale they'd given me was gone too quickly. I had two seats to myself; my mom had moved across the aisle to sit beside a man who kept smiling at her. Before she went she leaned close and told me this was the beginning of my real life. She wanted me to forget my father and make the decision to have my life begin now, in our new destination – Canada.

It was July 1973, I was ten, almost eleven and everything I knew about the world was about to change. My mother talked of her home country as a modern place where the streets were paved with gold. I would learn later that the gold was in men's pockets and my mother would loan herself to them for a while and live off their gold. I think she always believed she could settle but it never worked. My father must have been very special for her to move from Canada to Scotland and be with him, or maybe when she fell pregnant with me while she was on holiday in Britain she just decided to stay. I don't know. I've never asked either of them to tell me the real story about what happened.

The time it took between leaving our home in Kilmarnock to touching down in Vancouver was almost two days with time changes, flight delays, and waiting at Vancouver airport because my mother's friend was late arriving to pick us up. It was hot there, too; I remember the heat very well. There was so much sun. In the first two days, there was sun from morning till nighttime. I was from Scotland; the only sun that I knew about was maybe coming tomorrow after it stopped raining, or from time to time surprising us with a clear day. I think now about the major world events that were happening in the early seventies and none of it mattered to me. The only thing that mattered was that I'd been born in Scotland so the man at the customs area at Vancouver airport declared me a landed immigrant, whatever that meant. This was my new life.

My mother's friend who picked us up at the airport held onto her and swung her in the air. I didn't know what that meant but it didn't seem right. He made me say things like, "No problem," and then he interrupted me and told me that I sounded Canadian now. He was harmless I suppose but I had a weird feeling in my stomach; I just didn't know what it was.

My mother dismissed her friend after he dropped us off at a motel. He wanted to stay and help but she had other plans I suppose. We lay side by side in adjoining beds and I stared up at the ceiling. There were sparkles in the ceiling material. It was like looking at stars in the sky and when my mother turned out the light the sparkles shone even brighter in the dark. Maybe everything was going to be all right. I was scared but I was optimistic, too. Scotland had been about trying not to be the last boy picked for the football team and avoiding fights. Maybe she was right; this could be my life from now on. My mother snored soundly as I stared at the sparkles. The Kilmarnock schoolyard fights were about getting into position and grabbing the other boy's hair, then pulling it down and kicking him in the head. I had been kicked in the head once and I didn't like it. And

I'd been punched in the stomach and winded. That was before I'd decided to become a secret agent, though. This would be different. This would be about carving out a new identity and being something. At ten, almost eleven, I needed a change.

When I woke up in the morning and the sick feeling in my stomach was still there I knew what it was; I knew what was missing and I changed my mind about Canada. Two days later I pulled those sparkles out of the motel room ceiling while my mother was outside talking to someone. I ripped the stucco finish apart and let it drop onto the bed, sabotaging my mother's plans of having a perfect Canadian son. She immediately arranged to have me sent back to my father in Scotland. It didn't matter to me; I knew I'd be okay. I knew my dad would look after me and so would Scotland.

Growing up, I spent my summers in Canada with my mother and those were adventures, but I knew I'd always have my dad and I'd always have Kilmarnock to go home to. When I finally moved to Canada as a young man to attend university, it wasn't to leave my dad. I just thought I was old enough to handle the sick feeling in my stomach, and I wanted to reinvent myself once again. It had nothing to do with not wanting him. I always loved my father.

I stare down at my ledgers and the black and white numbers in the columns stare back at me. I've always found comfort in numbers. They don't change; they always stay the same. I take the letter out of my shirt pocket and read it again.

My Dear Son,

I hope this finds you well. I have had very little news of you in quite some time so I assume you're off saving the world. Please say hello to your family.

I'm writing to tell you that I will be unavailable for the next few months. My gentleman companion is an outdoor enthusiast and involved in a number of projects out of town this summer. We will be traveling nationally and perhaps even internationally. So do not worry about your mother as I am well. When I am back in circulation, I will contact you and then perhaps you will resolve to

communicate with me on a more regular basis.
Best,
Agnes

It's difficult to tell whether the letter was written before Terry's wife Jo paid for my mother's Romani friend's medical service or written afterward. My guess is that the letter was written after and that my mother made the connection of Jo to Terry and subsequently to me. She's always been very quick to ascertain those types of things. The letter, with its usual mix of brevity and guilt, was her way of telling me that he was not a gypsy-type, Romani person, and that she was okay. Even though I've read it several times already and shown it to Heather, I still laugh before folding it and putting it back in my pocket.

When I look out the window, the child is long gone. I say a silent prayer that her parents cherish her the way a child should be appreciated. The clouds are blocking out the sun now and even though it's still morning, it darkens the street. It doesn't matter. For a few moments I can still feel the warmth, the comfort. The empty feelings that I had in Canada as a child are long gone. I know where I'm supposed to be now. This is my town, my country. This is my home.

Chapter Twelve

I DON'T BELIEVE two people drift apart without some intent from at least one, or maybe even both of them. I don't think that can happen. I believe that somewhere along the line you make a conscious decision to travel the road alone. So much was happening and it was good, all of it. We were a couple making plans, and working together, but at some point, she decided to travel the road alone. Maybe I did the same and just hadn't admitted it to myself yet. It was her who got lost first though. It wasn't just her preoccupation with Barry at the school. That might have been something or it might have been nothing. It was her detachment. From the time we sat on either side of Emily when we landed in Scotland, I told her we were a team. It never felt like she accepted it, though. She said the words but she couldn't do it.

I could try to justify what I did by lying to myself that it was unresolved feelings that I had for Nan, or a love that was never allowed to grow but I know that isn't true. Back in primary school, we were young; we were only thirteen, too young to know what those things really were. I'm not sure if I believe that, though, because I still don't understand it. My heart jumped the same way when I saw her at forty as it did when we were thirteen-year-old kids. I see her jogging toward me or she'll be standing at our meeting place, waiting for our run, and she'll look over and I feel the same way, the exact same I did when I was thirteen. Does that mean you can pursue it? No, it does not. But I did. With Heather at home and Emily, I allowed it to happen. I made it happen.

I'd never been to her house. In fact, I'd rarely been up to the old Onthank Avenue since I was a schoolboy. It used to be all old houses and my travels never took me there. We vary our route because she wants to show me the old neighborhood. This is the real old neighborhood. These were the streets that tortured me. I'd walk home, hoping to avoid the little packs of boys who took delight in menacing the rest of us. Thirty years changes every place but not Onthank Avenue. There are still a couple of old houses, relics, she calls them, looming among the new apartment buildings. They've stayed the same while the land around them has changed. Toward the end of the road, there is still a small convenience store and a couple of low blocks of apartments.

"You won't recognize it, Malcolm. It must look different to you." She slows her pace and watches my reaction as she runs alongside me.

The sense of menace is gone but the desperation is still there. I can feel it seeping from the buildings.

"What happened to the people who lived in the houses? Where did they go?"

"The council sold their houses and changed them to high-density lots. That way they could build the apartments and fit more people in. There's still nowhere for the wee yins to play, though, that's the tragedy."

There are no people on the empty streets. They look cleaner than I remembered and the road is narrower, everything is smaller.

"I'm up here, further on." She picks up speed and turns around a corner in the direction of our old school. Within minutes we're standing beside a newer block of the same apartment buildings. "We moved my mom in here when she couldn't look after her house anymore and when Stuart passed I moved into her place to look after her. Then, I just stayed. It's small but it's all I need."

We stand outside. The building is whitewashed and looks cleaner than the old grey buildings that surround it. Flower pots with colorful plants hang over the edge of window boxes on some of the residences.

"Yours has flowers, I'll bet."

She smiles and points to a balcony on the third floor. "You're right. It's that one."

She leans over and stretches her legs against the curb, leaning down grabbing her knees. "Would you get lost if I left you here? Or can you find your way home?" She looks up at me with the brownest eyes I've ever seen and she flashes her innocent little girl smile.

I sigh and smile back. "I think I'll be okay."

She looks disappointed for a moment and then makes her way to the front door of the building. "Well, if you need a map just let me know and I'll draw something out for you."

I watch as her slender, curvy figure walks to the door. We aren't thirteen anymore.

She stops when she has the door open and calls back. "I'll see you tomorrow? Usual time?"

I do not move. "You shall."

She keeps the door ajar, watching me, half in the door and half still in the entranceway.

The seconds last forever. They feel like all the years that I haven't been here.

I walk toward her. When I reach her, she opens the door and lets me walk in. Then I follow her to the elevator. She pushes the button but still does not look at me. An older man comes out of the lift and eyes both of us up and down. He shakes his head and mutters. "Short pants on a day like this. The two of youse need your heads examined."

We hold our laughter until the man is gone and the sliding door of the elevator closes us in. She leans against one wall and covers her mouth, laughing. I walk toward her and kiss her for the very first time.

I follow her into the apartment but I see nothing other than her eyes, her hair, her body. I back into the door, closing it and I pull her toward me. Hurriedly, she pulls off her runners and then holds my face as I kiss her once more.

"I should shower. I'm sweaty." She rushes the words out between kisses and me holding her close.

"I don't think I can wait." I pull her t-shirt up over her head while we're gasping to each other.

She pulls me down the hallway and leads me into the bathroom.

"Come. Come in here, sweaty boy."

The water temperature switches from cold to scalding to warm again but I don't care. She has the whitest, softest skin. The spray from the shower turns to little drops and clings to her chest. She pulls a bar of soap from the ledge around the bathtub and starts soaping up her breasts. The snow-whiteness of the soap contrasts with her skin and the redness of her nipples.

"Good Scottish soap, this'll clean us up."

I help her by rubbing my hands over her chest and down her smooth, flat stomach and then between her legs. For a brief moment, I think of my home and my life, but I keep going. I do not stop. I don't allow the outside images to stay in my head.

She puts her arms around my neck and I pull her up and experience what I've wanted to do with her for years. I wanted to do it before I even knew what it was. I lift her and lower her over and over again. I hold her against the wall and think only of the pleasure, the way it feels, then the release, the long-awaited build up that I never knew I had. When she cries with satisfaction there are tears coming from her eyes and her mouth opens. She gasps and then takes in large breaths of air as the water continues to bounce off us.

She clings to me hard, her nails digging into my shoulders.

When we finish she turns away from me and I hold her from behind. She raises her head and lets the water wash over her and then steps gently over the ledge of the bathtub and out of the shower. I wait for a moment and then wash myself off. When I come out there's a towel on the vanity. I quickly dry myself and then put my sweaty t-shirt and shorts back on. She's sitting in the small living room that's off the hallway. She's wearing jogging pants and an oversized sweatshirt with the name of the Kilmarnock football team emblazoned on the front. She's sitting on the edge of the couch and looks up as though I've walked in on her unexpectedly. I stand there awkwardly. I've never done this before. I don't know what to do.

"I'm sorry, Malcolm. I was lonely. I get really lonely sometimes."

I walk toward her but she shakes her head, not permitting me to come closer. I stop in the middle of her small living room. "It was nice, really nice. You have nothing to apologize about."

She nods and smiles a smile that I've never seen before.

"You should go."

When I get to the door the logistics of what just happened occur to me. I just had unprotected sex with a woman who I used to know. I am going home to my partner who at some point may also want to have sex with me. I just cheated on Heather. It doesn't matter where we are or what this was, I just cheated on Heather.

She's at the end of the hall when I look back.

"Nan, we didn't use protection."

"I'm as barren as the desert, Malcolm and I haven't been with anyone since Stuart died. You have nothing to worry about."

I open the door and have a thought as I leave. "I'll see you tomorrow? Or the next day?"

The popular girl from school answers the awkward, shy boy. "No, not tomorrow. It might be best to leave it for a few days. Give me a few days. We'll run again soon."

I let the weight of the heavy door close behind me and I'm in the hall. I hear the deadbolt clicking locked a few seconds later. I've been pushed away once again. The hallway smells like someone has been cooking some vile concoction mixed with sweat. I sniff at myself but that's a different smell. This is old Scottish building smell

73

in a new building. I remember it. I take the stairs this time and walk down as quickly as I can. There's a woman shouting something to someone and I hear the clatter of metal and then a television is turned up loud. When darkness comes there will be other calls and threats. I've been here before; I know what this feels like.

It's unusually bright out and I squint into the sun when I get out to the path. I jog toward my house, feeling the cold from the morning air. Heather will still be at the school. Emily won't be home for a few hours. No one will know what I've done. I turn up the avenue away from the direction of our old school. I just had sex in a shower with a girl I fantasized about in primary school. It was a moment of weakness, but it was not. I've watched her as we ran together. I've watched her when we stopped at the top of the hill in the Dean Park. It's always been on my mind. Always. There was no moment. It was a plan. I always knew what I wanted to do. And she did, too. She was lonely and I was there. That's all it was.

When I see our house, my heart feels heavy and there's a tightness in my throat. This is the house that I call our home. This is where the three of us live. My father is two streets away and Hardly is across the road. I've dirtied it, but in spite of it all, in spite of everything I've done, there's a feeling building within me and I don't want it to stop. I can't stop myself from wondering when I'm going to see her next and if we're going to have sex again.

Chapter Thirteen

MY DAD'S CONDITION becomes worse. We make a date and invite him for dinner and he either doesn't come or he arrives two nights early. From time to time he's cantankerous and he's becoming more secretive all the time. He's not the man who invited us into his home five years ago. The strong man who welcomed my family to Scotland and held me and told me it was good to have me back is not here anymore.

The calls to our home continue. They're from men with strange accents or friendly women who ask for my father by his first name. I can't determine whether the accents are European or African. When I ask what business they have with Alex Wilson the conversation is always abruptly terminated. One day, we receive a call from a man with a posh, as we called them when we were children, English accent.

Heather hands me the phone and covers the receiver. She shakes her head when she gives it to me. "Let's get the police involved. This is too much. Maybe they can trace the call."

I pretend that I'm him, answering that I am indeed Alex Wilson of Kilmarnock. After a short conversation, they ask me to renew my pledge to ensure my forthcoming greatness. I know what's coming next. They don't just ask for money. They ask me to continue sending money. When I hang up the phone I think of the incident with the boys when they took Dad's newspaper. He'd been quite resigned to the fact that he didn't have the fight in him anymore. He isn't an old man, though. He still seems strong and agile; an able man in his sixties. Maybe Flora is right. It's been building over the years, and it's getting worse. I can't just let it happen, though. I need to find a way to make it stop.

I call Joy, his lady friend, and try to set up a visit. Maybe he needs to get away and talk to someone his own age. My call is intercepted by her daughter and when I ask after her mother's health she tells me that her mom is experiencing a similar malady. Before I can speak about my dad, Joy's daughter Lyla tells me about her mother's forgetfulness and how they're at the point where they feel the need to constantly monitor her. Before she left, my father told me she was acting strangely and seemed to be indifferent to him. Maybe it wasn't indifference, maybe it's the same affliction my dad has. I make a plan with Lyla to bring my dad down to England to visit in a month or two and hang up the phone no further ahead.

Heather has her up and down days. She enters these black periods but lately it's been better. She's working nights on a school project, and there's a renewed vigor about her. Her skin is flushed and she's enjoying the company of the children. Her duties as a teacher's assistant mean she has to do the grunge work. She's the one who makes sure everything is put away after each project and when it isn't done by the children, she does it herself. Or she helps monitor them when the class takes their weekly trips to the Dick Institute, our local library. The proud old building sits on the outskirts of my running route. It's been a local institution for years. I remember the trips I made myself each week to pick out an Enid Blyton novel or when required, some Dickens or Robert Louis Stevenson. She takes her responsibilities seriously and if there's a problem with the library administrator or if one of the teachers who she assists needs a project completed after class, she does it without complaining. In a way, it's not so different from when she worked for Terry back in Canada.

When she worked for my friend as his assistant, she often liaised with sales people and Terry would refer to them as children. She doesn't talk much about the kids but I imagine she can relate to all of them, especially the kids from the rougher areas, the kids who are on the outside looking in.

The night that Hardly went off the rails began well. I walked over and picked up Dad for dinner so he wouldn't forget that he was coming. We walked back together and talked about the dismal state of Scottish football and wondered if there would ever be any great players pulling on the jersey again. Heather had made a fish supper but cooked him some turnips, or neeps, and served them on the side. Emily, of course, couldn't resist commenting.

"They look like ground up sawdust, Grandad. How can you eat that, and the color - it looks like a vegetable that's been plugged into a power socket."

"This is what I grew up on. I had a cousin who had a farm in Inverness and she'd send them down to me. Anything covered in dirt that comes from the ground is good for you."

Heather dishes a small spoonful onto Emily's plate. Her teenage eyes bore a hole through her mother. She doesn't seem to recall chiding me to eat them back in her softer, pre-teenage years.

"You cannot be serious."

"A spoonful, Emily. It won't kill you."

My dad looks across the table at her. "Okay. We'll do it together. Get ready."

Emily smiles back. She can't resist him. "It's not fair, you like them."

"I didn't say that. I said I eat them but I've never liked them. They're disgusting."

Emily snorts out a laugh but he cuts her short. "Come on. Fill your fork, let's go."

She does as she's told and they start piling the turnip into their mouths. It's impossible not to laugh at the two of them. I feel like we should be observing and not commenting, but Heather pipes up.

"I worked hard on that, you two. Slow down and try to enjoy it."

When the last of the neeps are gone from Emily's plate she looks over at her mother who is sitting across from me, in front of her own plate.

"Actually, it tastes different this time. It's not the same taste that it usually is."

Her mother smiles across the table. "I added brown sugar; it helped change the taste a bit, didn't it?"

The door opens and Hardly comes in, barely balancing his one side on his cane. He pauses when he sees us all at the table, and I can smell the liquor on him. He's wearing his old army tunic, and it's tighter on him than when he served. Usually, he avoids my father's eyes when he's liquored up but this time he's in a bad way and he begins rambling, looking at all of us, sweat rolling down his cheeks.

"She's gone. Her bags are gone, her clothes, everything. And this is all she left, a note, saying she'll call me. She's gone back to Aberdeen; I know she has. I'm going back there. I'm going to get the lads and go after her."

We're all up, even Emily, but it's my dad who gets to him first.

"You're no going anywhere, lad. Come and sit."

He's the only one who Hardly will listen to. Hardly has been down over Flora in the past but I've never seen him like this. He's shaking, in an almost manic state. My father sits him in our living room and urges the rest of us to keep eating our dinners. It's a small house and even though he's murmuring to him we can all hear the words. Somehow he seems to know more about Hardly's problem than the rest of us. He tells him about a work mate he had years ago and how the alcohol got a hold of him. The only thing he could do to fight it was total abstinence. When Hardly argues that it has nothing to do with the booze, my dad disagrees and tells him it has everything to do with the booze.

"I just need to see her, to get her back."

My dad gives him the same firm stare he gave the two of us when we were young boys. "Start with yourself, son. Start looking after your own self and then you can see about Flora."

My friend nods to him but his eyes are saying that he doesn't believe it.

Once I've finished my dinner, I join them in the living room. Emily follows, and sits close to me, hanging on every word, worried about her Uncle Harry while Heather clears the table, listening and watching us. It's a family problem and Hardly is our family.

"What about your meetings, mate?" I ask. "What about going back to those, they seemed to help." He attended meetings with other alcoholics for a while when Flora began to stray. They helped him stay sober for a long time.

He gets angry when I make the suggestion. "It's like being in the Twilight Zone, Malcolm. They say the same things over and over again, night after night, and each time they act like they've never heard it before. And when they meet each other they act like it's been years since they saw each other even though it was just the week before. I can't go back there."

He's sweating more now. He's jonesing for that next drink. I've seen him go through this before. His eyes dart around the room.

"I'm going to go to Aberdeen. I want to see where Walter is buried; I've never made it up there. I'll pick up Dougie and Larry on the way, and get the old outfit back together. Then I'll find her."

He lost Walter, his soldier friend, in a battle in Ireland, the same battle where he lost part of his leg. His friend was Flora's brother. That's how they met each other. Unfortunately, there's no hope that his old outfit will be getting back together. He seems to have forgotten the drunken phone calls he made when he discovered that his friend Larry had moved abroad and the ringleader of the bunch, Dougie, had just plain disappeared after one last tour of Ireland. No one has seen him in years. I don't want to deflate him, though, not tonight. So I give him something.

"That's a good idea. We'll leave tomorrow."

Everyone looks at me as though I've just laid an egg in the middle of the floor. Then my dad lays his own egg.

"Aye, and I'll come, too. We'll do a road trip."

Emily tries to join in. "And, me, too. I'll come to look after you, Uncle Harry."

Heather and I speak at the same time, something we haven't done in a long time. "School."

"Um, okay, no need to get aggressive about it."

I steal a smile at the girl who I ran across the world with and she smiles back and asks me, "Are you sure you can get away? Don't you have clients?"

"I'll reschedule. It'll be fine. We'll go up north. Can you come? Can you get away from school? We could all go."

Emily is encouraged again and tries to speak but her mother answers immediately. "No, there are some things I need to take care of. I'm sorry, I can't. Em and I will stay here."

Hardly hasn't spoken. He seems perplexed by the whole thing.

My dad takes control. "Then, it's decided. I'll take my two boys up north for a wee trip to the Highlands. We'll pay our respects to Walter's parents and visit his grave. And you will dry out, lad."

Hardly agrees and when he tries to leave and go back to his own place and his booze, Emily steps in. "You'll stay here tonight, Uncle Harry. We're going to look after you."

If I had suggested it, he would have argued but he never disagrees with Emily. The couch is made up and we make him as comfortable as we can while I arrange to pick up my dad in the morning from his home.

I sit beside him on a chair while he sleeps on the couch. The house is dark and we're settled when I hear the noise. It's Emily's door. I know the squeak well. When it doesn't close again after a few minutes I get up to see if she's okay. She's sitting at the top of the stairs with her head resting on the banister and her arms folded in front of herself. She looks up when I get close.

"He was mumbling in his sleep. I just wanted to see if he was okay."

I sit beside her and we watch my friend down below. He's in a full sitting position now, oblivious to Emily and me. His eyes are closed and he seems to be asleep while he's having an extremely animated discussion with someone. Emily switches positions and leans against me, laying her head on my shoulder.

Hardly speaks to the dead air in front of himself. "You scare me when you sleep with your eyes open like that. It's like you're watching me from inside your head."

There's a pause and Hardly nods over and over while he listens to his invisible companion. I put my arm around Emily and she huddles in even closer.

"Aye, I know. Listen." He waits and I understand. He's dreaming about something that happened when he was in the army. He's reliving it. He shakes a little as he whispers. "They're still down there. I'm not waiting. I'm not going to wait for the bastards to come up this time."

His face is wet and there's saliva running from the corner of his mouth. He pushes himself up completely from the couch. Emily and I are both up. Hardly's eyes are still closed. He's forgotten that he's missing his leg and he's going to swing out onto the floor. My long legs allow me to reach the bottom of the stairs in two strides, and Emily is just behind me. He doesn't need us. The voice that only he can hear has calmed him. He stops and lies back down and lays his arms by his sides.

"Okay, okay. We wait; we keep waiting for now."

After a moment he's still again. His eyelids twitch once, twice and then he seems to be asleep.

I gently hold Emily back from him. She wants to comfort him but she understands, too; it's better to let him sleep. We watch him for a moment until he's breathing deeply and then I lift her up into my arms. As she's gotten older and taller I've gotten older, too, but my father's genes are strong and I have no trouble lifting her up as she drapes her arms around my neck. I tiptoe up the stairs then push her bedroom door open with my toe and deposit her on her bed.

"I wish I could come. I should be looking after him. I could look after all of you."

I think of battles won and battles lost and I wonder how important school days really are. "Let me talk to your mother. If it's only for a couple of days then maybe you can come. You probably should come."

She kisses me on the cheek and says nothing.

"I said I'll try. Just try." I tuck the covers around her and wonder how many more times I'll get the opportunity to do this as she grows older and inevitably leaves us all behind. "Go to sleep, Em. I'll keep Uncle Harry company."

When I close her bedroom door behind me I think about the day in Nan's apartment and I feel sick. Nothing feels the same as it once did. In a perverse way, I have no fear of being found out but I do fear losing what just happened. I look at our closed bedroom door and consider going in and telling Heather everything. I don't though. I'm not ready. Maybe I never will have the courage to tell her. When I'm back in the living room I sit beside my friend and look up the stairs at the life I've jeopardized, the life I always wanted.

Chapter Fourteen

I MANAGE TO lean back in the old chair and position it so that I can rest my long legs on the end of the couch that Hardly's shorter stature doesn't quite cover. His eyes open briefly and he almost smiles. Then he goes back to sleep, the conversation with his invisible companion now over.

I doze for a while but when he stirs, I draw in my breath and wake up. When I glance to the top of the stairs Heather is half a step back in the hallway, in the darkness. She's been watching me and smiles as we share a moment. I'm leaving her, and possibly Emily, too, alone tomorrow. I think about what Terry told me; he can't confirm that her father is dead. I can't tell her, not now. Not yet. Terry will find a way to confirm, he's good at that. I saw John Postman die; he isn't alive. Our eyes stay on each other for a few seconds and our expressions are frozen onto our faces. I drop my legs to the floor and start to make my way to the stairs to join her but she raises the palm of her hand, telling me to stop. She blows me a kiss and goes back to bed and I remember. I remember other times, better times.

My father's memory is in perfect working order when he awakens our household a few hours later at seven am. For a moment it's like having my old dad back. He remembers why he's at our house and he knows where we're going. Then, when I take a closer look at him, I notice that he's wearing at least three shirts under his jacket and the top shirt is his pajama top. I don't understand what's happening to him. He's struggling with something; I just don't know what it is.

The sun streams through the living room curtains as we watch Hardly shake and complain while he deals with his hangover. Dad has the kettle on and is boiling water for tea while Hardly makes his way to the bathroom, half bent over. When Emily sneaks downstairs, she gives me an expectant look and a smile, wondering whether I've convinced her mother to excuse her from school for a couple of days.

Before I can answer Heather appears at the top of the stairs and looks down at Emily, who's still dressed in her nightclothes. Heather gives her daughter the same protective mother look that most of the world has had to experience from time to time. I can't read Heather's face properly. I don't know if she's having one of her good days or if she's struggling again.

Emily speaks quickly before her mother can say anything. "I've been thinking and I have to tell you that I disagree with your thoughts on whether I should go to Aberdeen." She looks at me and briefly considers whether to use my approval as a bargaining chip, but then decides not to. "I think you should reconsider."

Heather bounds down the stairs, fully dressed and looking especially fresh-faced for such an early hour. There's a brightness on her face, and I can tell. She's having one of her good days. She answers her daughter and looks at me at the same time.

"I've been thinking, too and I believe you might be right, Em. If you commit to making up the work at school when you get back, I think you should be able to go. Malcolm?"

Emily looks more stunned than I feel. I watch Heather as she moves around the kitchen, giving my father a peck on the cheek and pulling some slices of orange from the refrigerator.

"I thought it over, Malcolm. I'm sorry that we couldn't talk about it last night. If you disagree let me know but it might be good for her to spend some time with you guys."

Emily is excited now. "Yes, I'll make up the work, no problem. And I'll look after them."

Heather has a glass of juice in her hands and smiles at Emily. "Yes, you will look after them. I know you will."

I'd love to have her with us and I know my dad and Hardly will, too. And I didn't even have to convince Heather.

"I wish you were coming, too. It won't feel the same without you."

Emily interrupts me. "So, I'm going? This is brilliant. I have to call Fiona and Lorraine to let them know that I won't be at school. Luckily, I packed just in case you saw the logic in my plan."

She pauses and looks at her mother. They share a moment

"And Mom…"

"I know Em. I'll be fine. There are no more ghosts."

Heather shakes her head and laughs as we watch Emily racing back upstairs, the portable phone gripped firmly in her hand. "I can't, Malcolm. There's too much going on right now. Take the mobile, the one that Terry sent us. Phone me and let me know what's happening."

Two years ago Terry sent us one of his latest inventions, or an invention that one of his young protégés had designed. It's a mobile phone that can be used anywhere in the world. And he set it up so that it homes in to him. So he's always accessible to us. At first, it was a novelty and we used it from time to time as we made our worldly trips to the school or football pitch, but for the past few months it's stayed on our living room counter, plugged in and unused.

When she reappears from her bedroom, Emily takes Hardly across the street and helps him pack up his stuff, making sure he doesn't pack any liquor. An hour later, with my father pushing us toward the door, we're on the road. Emily makes each of us take a bottle of water and a bag of potato chips or crisps as she's come to call them in the Scots way and Heather slips the mobile phone into my pocket. She's rushing to get to her school children but she stops to hug me and holds on a little bit longer than she usually does.

My dad insists that Hardly sit in the front while I drive and Emily sits with her grandfather in the back seat of our small car. It doesn't make sense. Hardly is the shortest but I think my dad wants to spend some time visiting with Emily. I drive the car down past the Dean Park and through the old part of town and even though it's earlier than our usual time, my eyes instinctively search the sidewalks for Nan out running. I haven't seen her since the day in her apartment. None of my passengers notice as I look down the park entrance toward the trail, and no one should. None of them know of our friendship. Kilmarnock is a small town but if you're careful there are still secrets that can remain private.

Hardly and my father take turns dozing and Emily reads from her comic books, chuckling softly from time to time. When she was younger my father gave her an ancient stash of *Beano* and *Dandy* comics that had belonged to me as a boy. She immediately became a fan, reading about the characters I grew up with. I think of how it felt the night before when I carried Emily up the stairs and how good it was to have Heather smiling down at me.

I lost Heather once. When we were chasing down Emily, back in Ontario, she disappeared. Those were different times, different circumstances but the feeling I have now is similar. She's here, but she's not. Or maybe it's me. Maybe I'm just trying to justify what I did.

The same thoughts keep going through my head and I know I'm the guilty one. You don't plan on it happening. You don't sit down and decide that you're going to hurt another person. And I don't believe it just occurs either; I won't use that excuse. Somewhere inside me, I saw where the road was leading and I took it. I made the choice.

If anyone tells you that they had an affair and it happened suddenly, they're lying. I know because it doesn't work like that.

When we moved to Kilmarnock there were so many things right about our lives. We had a family connection that neither Heather nor I had experienced in a long time. I hadn't had it since I lived as a young lad with my father and she hadn't felt it since her mother was alive. With my dad living a couple of streets away and Hardly and Flora across the road, we had a feeling of security that was unfamiliar to us. At first, we saw lots of them but then at some point it was as though they'd had a private chat and decided to back off a bit. I asked Hardly one day if he and my dad had spoken, and whether they'd decided it best to leave us to ourselves for a bit. When we were young boys in short pants, he would either have answered me or at least given me a look from which I could decipher the truth, but as a grown man who'd already lived the type of life in the military that few of us will ever see, he developed a solemn mannerism that gave away very little.

"It's the right thing to do, mate. We're close by when you need us. We just won't be sitting on your doorstep for a wee while." He'd somehow developed this expression where half of his mouth would crinkle into a smile and he'd give me a wink at the same time. And he managed to do all of this while he was still speaking.

"So, the two of you did talk then, you and Dad?"

"A closed mouth catches no flies, Malcolm." And then he gave me his funny expression again. He never had that when we were growing up but then again he never had much to smile about in those days.

Things developed naturally. I'd had nothing to do with children other than the fact that at one point, thirty years ago, I was one. Emily was different, though. She was a wise old soul in a child's body and that was something I could relate to. I'd grown up being exposed to things that most children wouldn't see until they were adults so in a way I felt I could empathize with Heather's daughter. It took some time but after a while her quiet periods became less and less and she felt comfortable enough to be herself, to be a little girl, around us. Heather and I consciously decided that we'd treat her like a normal little girl, as though nothing had happened. Maybe that was a mistake. Maybe we should have talked it out or had her speak to someone but we never did.

When she was younger she would make childish sounds as she was moving from the kitchen into the small backyard of our home, puffing her cheeks out and blowing a little girl's noise. And then if she saw me she would stop and ask an adult question. It amazed me that she could go from her childlike world to asking why the refrigerators in Scotland were backward from the ones in Canada or why our backyard was smaller than the yards in Canada. We'd been in Kilmarnock about three months when the questions began to be asked more frequently.

"Don't you like our yard, Emily? It's almost exactly like the yard I had when I was a boy."

She answers immediately and I feel bad for asking right away. "I like it. I was just wondering."

I'd have done anything for her in that moment, anything she asked.

I open the old wooden doors of the pantry and grab an empty glass jar from the shelf. "Come and I'll show you something." She pauses, eyeing me suspiciously. "Okay, you sit on the back step and I'll show you what I used to do when I was your age."

I take the jar over to the small patch of dirt that we have at the back of the yard. She's only a few feet from me and I can feel her eying me intently. I place the jar on the grass beside the dirt and then I take a flat rock and dig up a little bit of the dirt from the vegetable garden where nothing grows because we don't plant any vegetable seeds. That's all it takes. She runs from the steps and comes over to investigate.

"Buried treasure."

"Nope."

"Yes, Malcolm, buried treasure." Her mouth is a perfect "O" shape and she holds it that way and watches as I dig around in the dirt.

"Nope, no buried treasure."

"Vegetables from the garden, then?" She keeps watching me digging at the dirt as she speaks.

"Nope, still wrong."

Then I see one.

I pick up the worm with the flat rock and drop it into the jar.

"Ooooooo. That's so gross."

She backs away a little but keeps her eyes on the jar, not wanting to be too far from the action.

"When I was your age, my dad would take me fishing and we'd use worms as bait. It would be my job to dig up enough worms for all the hooks on the fishing rods."

She comes closer again, and taps on the side of the jar. The worm, in its worm-like fashion, ignores her and keeps slithering around trying to find a way out of the jar.

"We can find a few and put them in the jar then take them over to my dad's if you want. Maybe he'll take us fishing."

She smiles and hunches herself down on her knees, staring at the dirt, watching for movement.

"We won't eat the fish though will we, Malcolm?"

"Not if you don't want to. We can catch them and then throw them back into the water."

She nods, agreeing, and takes the rock and starts digging, looking for another worm while I think about what my father's frugal, Scottish face is going to look like when he has to throw a perfectly good fish back into the river.

Somewhere along the passing miles Hardly has realized that there's no way we can connect with Dougie or Larry, his old army mates. "We'll go to Flora's parent's house. She'll be there. I have the address." He holds up a small piece of paper between his fingers.

I glance at the rear view mirror and Emily nods at me. She would have helped him locate it earlier in the morning when she accompanied him to his house. For all her teenage posturing and almost-rebelling she's still the same gentle soul she was when she was ten. That will never go away.

When I was a child and we occasionally traveled around Scotland, short distances took hours to cover. Now, with the motorways or major highways, the country has shrunk and traveling from south to north takes far less time. After talking about the weather and admiring the scenery, my passengers and I go into our own personal trances. I watch as the signs go by and I remember the hug Heather gave me before we left and then I think of the task I've given Terry when he told me he couldn't find proof that her father had died. It feels heavy, all of it, but I suppose all of my traveling companions are carrying their own weights.

"Castle." Emily sees it first and calls out. My dad echoes her while Hardly puts his hands on either side of his head.

"Aye, it's another castle. There's a few of them here, you don't need to yell."

Dunnottar Castle sits on the outskirts of Aberdeen. It's one of the most striking and picturesque castles in the country. It's long been a favorite of mine and I promised Emily that we would stop.

I slow down and Hardly lets go of his head. He draws the words out and speaks in the broadest Scottish accent he can manage. "It's fine, Malcolm. Let's go see the old Scottish castle."

My dad is wide awake now as I pull into the parking lot. "Everybody should get to experience Dunnottar. Come on, let's go."

There are only a few other cars and we can see people walking along the road back from the castle. Hardly and I sit in the car as Emily and my dad march up the path that leads to the ruins of the old stone structure.

We laugh as we watch them, each trying to talk over the other as they excitedly reel off what they know of the historic place.

It's the first opportunity I've had to talk to him alone since he stumbled into our living room the night before, other than when he was fast asleep. "What are you going to say to her if we find her up here, mate?"

He pauses and stares out the windshield for a while before answering me. "I don't know. I was angry and the drink didn't help. I know that. I feel like I have all these paths in my life that are cut off, they're over. Maybe she's one of them. Maybe the old man is right."

I laugh. "Of course he is. He always is."

"Maybe I need to make it about me and not her. I still don't think it's just the booze but I suppose that would be a start."

He's right but he doesn't need to hear that. I just sit and listen.

He keeps looking out the window, talking. "Aye, that would be a start. Again."

When we were children in the classroom, he was picked on because he was the smallest, and the masters and the other kids thought he was the weakest. Old Master Hextall from our primary school was ruthless as he bullied him. They were all wrong, though. He's not weak; he's the strongest person I've ever met.

"Do you remember when we climbed up the Burns monument and stood beside the statue? We felt like we were looking down on everybody."

He shakes his head and coughs in laughter. "What the hell made you think of that?" He can't stop laughing now. "Yes, we used to like climbing things, didn't we? We had no choice, we needed places to hide."

"I know, but listen. We were wrong. We don't have to climb. We just need to be. That's all we need. We don't need to look down on anything."

He pipes up before I can finish; his face serious now. "I don't have a clue what that means. Not a clue. But I do know one thing." He pauses and forces a smile out. "You're turning into your faither, Malcolm Wilson. Yes, you are so."

I'll take it. I'll take that compliment all day long. "I think some of him must have rubbed off on you, too. We can't escape from the old bugger."

I can see him in the distance, standing proudly and pointing to something in the distance, showing Emily his Scotland.

"Go, Malcolm, I'll sit here. I'm fine, right as rain."

By the time I pay at the entrance gate and reach the two of them, Emily is ready to tell me why Dunnottar Castle is so important.

"You have to understand that this castle has no double-pane windows. There is no stucco siding on the inner walls. Nothing has been rebuilt. What you're seeing is exactly how it was back in the ninth century."

I remember hearing the same lecture years ago, and I know exactly where she heard it. My father is smiling and nodding, pleased with himself. A young couple walks down the narrow passageway that leads to the uppermost part of the structure. Emily looks at my dad. "Grandpa, are we allowed to go up there?"

He points at me, deferring, and Emily smiles in my direction. "Dad?"

My Scottish accent seems to be getting stronger as the cold wind blows off the water and around the castle walls. "Aye, go, but be careful."

My dad and I walk to the edge of the cliff. The wind sweeps spray from the ocean water up onto our faces. We stand that way for a few moments until we hear Emily calling to us from the top of the castle. She waves and then looks out in the same direction that we're facing. My dad's face is soaked and I touch his elbow to try and get him to walk back from the edge a bit.

"I'm fine. It's healthy, it's good for you."

I stand closer to him, trying to shield him from the cold.

"I went to the doctor, Malcolm. He says I've got a bit of a problem with my memory. He gave me some pills but I'm a bit reluctant to take them."

I look down at him.

"I know, yes, I will take them. There's going to have to be some changes I suppose. This getting old isn't much fun, son."

We turn and Emily is walking toward us. Her face is flushed and she's smiling, alive. I can't stop staring at my dad. I start to speak but he cuts me off. "It's okay, I know. I'll take the pills. I have to try something, and it's better than the alternative. I know that."

When we get back into the car, Hardly has his arms folded. "The lot of you are nuts. Do you realize what the temperature is out there? Youse are off your heids."

We're not, though. We're alive and the stop helped all of us deal with the weights we're carrying. This explains some of what's going on with my dad. Maybe this is only the beginning but at least there's a way to deal with it now. I should have been with him. I should have suggested that he go to his doctor. It doesn't matter, though. We know what he has to do. I'll have him taking those pills even if I have to administer them to him in his sleep. This is a good thing. Emily leans forward, regaling her Uncle Harry with the little bit of history she read from the plaques around the castle. And my dad sits beside her, smiling, and content. Things will be better now. I can tell.

Chapter Fifteen

WE KEEP THE door closed during our morning meetings but the rest of the staff knows that we're in there. They must, but we don't care. Barry always looks the same. With his brightly-coloured shirts, jet-black hair, and wide sideburns he looks like he'd be more comfortable living twenty years ago. He's different, even a little eccentric, and if it wasn't for the way he speaks the children would probably love him. They keep their distance, though, the older ones sniping to the younger children that he's not one of them. He has one of those unusual Scottish accents that I exclaimed about to Malcolm and his father years ago. He's English. During one of our first meetings I couldn't stop smiling while he chattered quickly and poured tea into our cups.

"You're laughing at me. Did I say something funny?"

"No, it's just that you're English. I think?"

"Birmingham. The accent has stuck. I'll always have it."

"They allow you to stay here, though, that's good."

He laughs back at me. "Yes, I had to learn how to say 'aye', promise not to talk football or politics and eat the occasional plate of tatties and mince. Then they renew my resident's permit every six months. Now, how did you sneak in with your...Canadian accent?"

I don't know if he knows my history of moving from Canada to Scotland. Maybe he does and he's being coy. "That's very good. Most people think I'm American."

He smiles and doesn't elaborate. We stay quiet for a few minutes. Sometimes we do that. We just sit and drink our tea and let our thoughts settle. That's one of the ways he's helped me.

When Malcolm and Emily made plans to go with Hardly and his dad, I knew exactly what I was going to do. Barry and I had talked about it, and it was time. I find the building right away. It's between an old, stone church and a fast-food restaurant. It's in the opposite direction from the school but the bus route was pretty straightforward. Barry said he'd meet me in the parking lot but I didn't want that. It knew it would be easier if I went in alone. I check in at the reception desk and wait, just as we agreed. A young woman is sitting across from me and smiles as though she knows exactly why I'm here. I'm sure she doesn't but then again she could be here for the same reason I am.

When I called to make the appointment, they told me it was going to be weeks before I could get in but Barry's name opened the door. He and the doctor were old friends and they managed to get me in that day.

I expect the doctor to be a kindly old fellow because in my mind they always are, but he isn't. He's about my age. Barry and he went to school together so I should have anticipated that he would be younger.

He starts by talking about Barry, not as his patient, but as his friend. "He always had my back. He had his own troubles but he got through them by helping other people. He still is." He sits back in his chair and smiles at me. He doesn't have Barry's loud taste in shirts, preferring a more conservative grey with a navy tie showing through the V-neck of his sweater.

I look around the office and sure enough there's a long, white lab-coat hanging on a hook behind the door. He's watching my gaze and comments right away. "Aha, you found it. Now you know."

There's something about him that's making me relax. "Yes, you're a mad scientist."

"Guilty. I have test tubes hidden in every drawer. No evil assistant though, I'm afraid. That's my wife at the front desk. She keeps me in check."

I like him and even when he switches to his more professional demeanour, I still feel comfortable enough to tell him what's been going on in my head. He suggests that I have a complete physical examination from my family doctor but I know what he's thinking and I have to ask.

"The things I've told you, the symptoms, I've always had them. So regardless of what happens with the physical exam I probably have it, don't I? I probably have the same thing that Barry has."

I can tell that he doesn't want to say but he gives me a little bit. "We need to talk more, but based on what you've told me, if your family physician can't find anything physically wrong then yes, you are exhibiting symptoms conducive with bipolar disorder."

Before I can ask he cuts in. "It could also be related to something else." He sees the disappointment in my face. "But, if that is the case, and you're right, and we don't know if it is yet, bear in mind that these days this is a very treatable affliction. There's medication, and awareness is important, too."

I smile at him. "I'm not worried. I just want to know what it is. I always knew there was something wrong with me and if this is what it is, I'll deal with it." I surprise myself by realizing how much I sound like Malcolm.

The bus ride home and the walk to my house is a blur. I'll make the appointment with my doctor but I know what's wrong. It has to be this. Barry has described to me what goes through his head and it's too similar to not be the same thing. I say the words in my head "bipolar disorder" or its old name "manic depression." I know what's wrong with me, and it's something that's treatable.

The computer is flashing; I see the light from the living room. There's only one person who talks to us on the computer. I type in my password and Terry's face flashes up on the screen. It's been a few months since I've seen him and he looks different. There's a flash as the systems connect and it confirms that he can see me, too.

He smiles and it reminds me of happier days when I worked for him back in Canada. Terry is one of those brilliant, creative people who finds joy in so many things; he constantly seems happy. I always envied that about him. And I enjoyed my time living on the west coast, far away from all the trouble in my hometown.

"Heather, it's good to see you." He calls behind himself to his wife. "Jo, Heather answered; I told you I'd get them."

"Good to see you, too, Terry. You look tired. I'll bet you're working too hard. Isn't your assistant doing enough for you these days? Do you need me to come back and straighten things out?"

He laughs. "Oh, I miss you so much some days. You're welcome anytime."

He tries to keep speaking but I interrupt him before he can continue. "You've actually missed Malcolm. He's up north with Hardly, Emily, and his dad for a couple of days."

"That's okay, just pass this along to him; well it's for you, too."

Jo is calling something to him in the background but I can't hear what she's saying.

"Tell him that I'm going to Ontario. I still can't find confirmation of your father's death so I'm going myself. I'll message you both once I'm there and I'll let you know what I find. It's ridiculous that there are no…"

I don't hear him anymore. All of the positive energy from earlier has drained out of me as I slump back in the chair. My father isn't dead. I knew this. I knew it.

Jo is calling to him again. I don't know what she's saying, but I can hear the urgency in her voice as he looks back. I see her hand on his shoulder and then she lowers her face toward the computer screen. She knows that I didn't know.

She speaks in a firm tone. "Heather, talk to me."

I straighten up in my chair and try to recover. "Jo, can you guys please tell me what you know about this?"

Terry has realized it now, too. Jo nods but it's Terry who speaks. "There's a massive amount of land that's still in your family's trust. It's controlled by Charles Postman." "That's my uncle. He's the one who inherited my father's estate. Remember, I signed it all over to him. Your lawyer helped us."

"No, he didn't get it. Not all of it anyway. There's still some land that's being controlled by a third party."

I interrupt him. "Can you tell me what you know about his death, Terry? That's all I'm interested in."

Jo cuts in. "There's no record, Heather. Terry can't find out where he's buried. Nobody wants to talk to him on the phone and they're not even responding to our lawyer's emails. That's why he suggested that he go to Ontario. He'll spend a couple of days talking to people. You know what he's like, nobody will say no to him. He'll find out and we'll report back in a couple of days. I'm sure it's just a failure to communicate. It's not like we're talking about a different country. Last time I checked Ontario was still in Canada."

She's still speaking but I don't really hear her. I take the little mouse in my hand and run the cursor around the screen. Malcolm's been working on this, asking questions, but he should have told me. He knew something was wrong and he kept it from me. The noises in the house might be real. I'm not imagining them.

"There's no need to go Terry. I'll book a flight and go myself. Don't worry." I smile as best as I can and cut them off. I keep talking before either of them can say anything. "And thank you for all that you've done. I'll let Malcolm know that you called." I click the link to close off the connection and I lean back in the chair.

Chapter Sixteen

HARDLY HAS HIS eyes half-closed and he looks like he's asleep, but when I pass the shop he sits up straight and calls at me to pull over. I take the next roundabout and turn around and park outside the flag shop. It's the only touristy-type establishment on the whole street It's one of those strange little businesses that only sells very specific items but somehow still seems to attract enough customers to survive. "Flags and Kites" is written in bold letters above the front door, and in smaller letters below it says "Established 1982." He's gone for barely a couple of minutes before stashing a small paper bag in his pocket and returning to the car. Whatever he's done is over. It doesn't look like they sell booze there so I'm not concerned. My dad has a calm, accepting look on his face and is still basking in contentment because we stopped at the castle. It's only Emily who looks at me questioningly. I shrug and we keep driving.

Hardly is more animated now and gives me directions. "Third roundabout, Malcolm, and then we should see it."

After stopping to eat and our diversion to Dunottar Castle, it's late in the afternoon and the sun is beginning to set. I think we're headed toward Flora's parents' house but we're not. As we get to the entrance I see a large stone sign over the road. Burned into it is "TRINITY CEMETERY."

Before I can ask, he speaks up. "It's the civilian cemetery but they have a large section of men and women who served. It's where Walter is. I remembered the name of the place, and the man at the flag shop gave me directions."

There's a quiet reverence about cemeteries. I pull the car into the parking lot, and I can feel the stillness even before we open the doors. We stand outside and stretch. Scottish cemeteries often have majestic stones commemorating even the most ordinary man or woman and Trinity is no exception. There are gravestones of impressive heights. Some of the newer stones, which I guess must have replaced the original markers, are placed in amongst the older stones, giving the rows a diverse look. Hardly and my dad seem to know what the protocol is, and for once Hardly doesn't need to be reminded to take his cane. He leans heavily on it as he and my father make their way toward a small building that's off to the side of the property. Emily and I walk toward one of the narrow roads that run up and down amongst the gravesites. We pause from time to time and read the names and dates on the stones. It's quiet as we walk up and down the first two rows. Emily's lips are moving as she stares. She's doing the math, too, just like me. We're calculating how old the deceased was when he or she passed away.

There are ranks in front of the people's names and on some, it tells of battles they were involved in. She's noticed it, too. "It seems like the whole cemetery is full of army, and military people."

"I don't think it is, honey. But they all seem to be in these first rows."

There are little metal holders in front of the stones, and some have flowers that have been left there. Some stick upward as though there's been a recent visitor while others are either empty or have wilted stalks hanging limply against the stones. Something makes us stop in front of a low marker that has a rusty, empty holder in front of it. We read the inscription and date together.

Emily covers her mouth and takes a step back, bumping into me. "He died when he was one year older than me. I'm almost his age. How is that possible?"

The man had a rank. He somehow must have enlisted when he was under age. She's looking at me for an answer.

"I don't know, Emily. Every stone in here has its own story."

She's shaking her head gently back and forth. "All of these people left someone behind."

There's an inscription below the young soldier's name but the stone is too dirty and I can't read it. Hardly and my dad are heading back toward the car and waving us over. It's too quiet. It's too much. I don't want to be here anymore. I don't want to be amongst the fallen, the gone. I want to pick up Emily and put all of us back into the car and preserve whatever is left of our family. I don't want Nan. I want confirmation from Terry's contacts that Heather's father is dead, and I want to be home. It doesn't work, though. I can't seem to move. I keep looking at the grave. I reach down and wipe at the inscription on the young man's stone.

All Good Men Must Fall.

There's no attribution and I don't recognize it. It seems like an odd saying and I wonder how it was relevant to the young man's life

Hardly and my dad are waiting for us. Emily pulls my arm and leads us toward the car.

There are two men, one young and one much older, standing outside the small building where Hardly and my dad just came from. They stand upright and they seem like they're ready to snap to attention as they look over at us, anxious to help.

Hardly holds up a map. "I have it here. They were very nice. The old man says he remembers Walter's service. He says it was raining hard and he remembers the day of the funeral. I don't know if he really does but it was nice of him to say that. I appreciate his effort."

My dad pats Hardly on the arm and Emily and I walk slowly behind the two of them as my friend tries hard not to limp. We walk in the opposite direction from the grave of the sixteen-year-old

103

soldier. We were in the section where military personnel are buried but we were at the other end from where Walter lies. There are numbers on flat, square stones at the end of each row. When we reach the appropriate row Hardly keeps going and my dad motions for the rest of us to stop. My dad looks as though he's tired all of a sudden. The walk up to the castle and confessing to me what was going on with his memory probably took a bit out of him. There are benches in between every few rows. I nod to him and the three of us head toward a bench to give Hardly some privacy.

After standing for a moment, he starts speaking. We can't hear him but it's as though he's explaining something to the gravestone as he occasionally waves around the free arm that isn't holding onto his cane. It was Walter he was speaking to last night in his sleep. I realize that now. His conversation goes on for a while as he leans on his cane and talks to his friend. Then he takes the little bag from his pocket that he got from the flag shop and places something on top of the stone. Then he does something I've never seen him do. He stands up straight and salutes. He's unsteady and Emily and I automatically lean forward so that we can rush to help him.

My dad's voice stops us. "Wait. He'll be okay. If he falls he falls. It's just grass and he doesn't have far to drop."

Emily and I look at my dad but he isn't laughing. "He has to do it on his own."

My friend does not fall. He stands bravely for a moment, and then he waves us over. When we get there we can see the tears in his eyes. There's a small American flag that he's placed on top of the stone.

He doesn't look at us when he explains. "Walter always wanted to go to America. He loved America. I thought he might appreciate a wee reminder."

His flag is more appropriate than flowers. This was a good thing to do. After standing silently for a few minutes, the four of us slowly walk back to the car. The two gentlemen from the little building wave to us and then go back inside.

When we get to the car I touch Emily's shoulder and tell her to wait outside. Her face is white and she looks lost. When my father and Hardly are settled into the back seat I put my arm around her and we walk a few feet away from the car. "Are you okay, Em?"

"I just don't get it. I really don't get it. All these soldiers are dead. And, that boy was so young."

I tell her what was told to me. I tell her because standing in the midst of so much sacrifice it feels truer to me today than it ever has before. "Because of what these people did, you and I have a chance to have a life. A good life."

"I know but, I just never."

She's right. Most of us will never know.

"Your Uncle Harry made sacrifices, too. You know that. You see him every day." I smile because it's been a reminder to me, too, a reminder that we should all experience from time to time.

"Yes, but now it's real."

It always was but I don't say it. I kneel down beside her and she puts her arms around my neck. As I hold her, I think of the inscription on the soldier's stone and I understand. I understand how it applies to all of us, not just him.

Hardly and my dad have been having their own private conversation while I was outside holding Emily but they seem to have finished now. After a moment, she lets go of me and we walk back to the car.

I don't really know where we're going. I look at my passengers in the rearview mirror and it's my dad who speaks.

"Head for home, Malcolm. We've done what needs to be done."

Hardly is in the back seat, beside him. Now I know what he and my dad were talking about. He has a settled, resigned look on his face. "It's up to Flora. If she comes home, she comes home. If she doesn't, I'll deal with it then."

My dad winks at me. He's been in control ever since we left Kilmarnock. Could the pills have started working already? Maybe he started taking them and was fibbing to me. Either that or the fates have allowed him a reprieve from his confusion and memory loss. I don't care why. I'm just grateful that it happened now, when we needed him most.

The mobile phone rings and before I can answer Emily grabs it. I can hear Heather's voice, loud, even from the driver's seat. Something has happened and this has turned into one of her bad days. She was fine this morning but that can change quickly; I've seen it before. It goes on too long, something else is wrong. As Emily listens her expression grows more and more tense. She holds the phone a little away from her face and looks at me as she speaks. "Mom, tell me why. Why are you going to Canada?"

I shut the car off and reach for the phone.

Emily keeps speaking. "Wait, though, talk to Dad. Wait."

I can't get a word in; Heather is already talking when I put the mobile phone to my ear. "Terry couldn't confirm, he doesn't know. So I'm booked for tomorrow night. I'm going. You should have told me."

It begins to make sense and I decide immediately. I have no choice. "Book for one more, Heather. I'm coming, too."

"I won't leave Emily here by herself, Malcolm. What if he's here? Maybe I was right about the noises. I could be. You need to stay here and look after her."

She spoke to Terry, she knows. And now the ghosts are back. Or maybe they never left. We could leave Emily with my dad or Hardly. Flora might even come back down to Kilmarnock and help look after her when she hears how important it is, but that won't be enough for Heather. I glance at Emily, wondering how she'd react to going back to the place we rescued her from. She knows what I'm thinking and mouths the words to me. "It's okay. I want to come."

She'll come. We're not going to hide from anything or anyone. "No, we'll take her. We'll do this together."

She continued talking in a low voice while I was answering her but she was listening, too. She finally stops and there's a brief pause. Dad and Hardly shift uneasily in the back seat. I reach over for

Emily's hand and she holds on to me for once. When Heather answers everyone in the car can hear her. "Okay, I'll book for the three of us. We'll leave tomorrow night. Come back here, Malcolm."

I suggest that Heather take my dad's spare key from our cupboard and spend the night at his house. I don't want her hearing any ghosts tonight and it'll be late before we get home. She won't do it. She's staying home.

We head down the motorway toward Dundee and then toward Glasgow and then home. Tomorrow night we'll leave for Woodbine, Ontario and look for a ghost. We're going back to where it all began.

Chapter Seventeen

HEATHER IS ASLEEP when we get home. Her pillows are propped behind her and she's sitting up as though she's been waiting for us. Emily kisses her mother on the forehead and she jolts awake and starts to lift herself up out of bed. Emily strokes her hair and she lies back down.

"I must have fallen asleep. I stayed awake as long as I could."

She looks at me standing in the doorway. She's angry that I didn't tell her, I can tell, but she nods as though everything is okay. "I'm glad you're home. Both of you."

She insists that I double check that Emily's window is locked. The latch is solid. Nobody is getting into our house. Poor Emily is so tired she can barely stand and immediately pulls her covers back and climbs into bed. Heather is still awake when I come back into the bedroom. I cut her off before she can speak. "We have a guard downstairs. I took Dad home but Hardly insisted on standing watch in the living room. He's been drinking tea for the past hour and he's got another flask beside him to help him stay awake."

She smiles.

"He says he's used to it and nobody will be getting in the house tonight."

"I believe him."

"I do, too."

She sits up while I'm getting undressed and she becomes more and more awake as she speaks. "I've been thinking more about whether we should take Em. She's doing so well here. Maybe she should stay here with your dad. I called Flora's number and left a message, and she got back to me a couple of hours ago. She's coming back; she's had a change of heart. Again. I think she just needed some time away from Hardly. She says she'll help look after Emily. She's probably on her way right now. With Hardly and Flora, she'll be fine. Flora says she won't let Emily out of her sight. I trust them to look after her."

"I think it's too late. We spoke a bit in the car while Dad and Hardly were dozing. She wants to go back, too. I don't think we'll be able to talk her out of it now."

We're in a situation where there are no right answers. I'm not sure she should be going but in a way, it might be better. This way she won't be avoiding a whole country for the rest of her life because of what happened when she was a child.

"You should have told me that you had Terry working on this. It might have helped."

"I thought I could get it handled. Then you wouldn't need to worry about it."

"You can't be everybody's hero, Malcolm. The world doesn't work like that."

I ignore her comment. I'm tired and there's nothing else I can say. When I get my body under the covers it feels for just a moment as though she's going to snuggle under my arm the way she used to. I lie on my back and wait, hoping, but it doesn't happen. She rolls over to the other side of the bed. Just when I think she's asleep, she speaks in a tired voice, her words slurred. I can't tell if she says that she didn't want to go without me or if she's saying she doesn't need me to go. It doesn't matter. This is my family and I'm going.

I've never needed seven or eight hours the way most people do. And even though the night before was unsettled as I balanced between a chair and the couch, I'm wide awake when I hear our front door being opened in the early hours of the morning. I can just make out the muffled voices of my father and Hardly. I slip out from the covers and pull on my shorts and T-shirt. Heather opens her eyes once I'm dressed.

"Really?"

"I need to clear my head, a run will help. I'll be back in half an hour."

"Don't be long. I need to go into the school this morning."

It's my turn to let my mouth hang open in exclamation. "Isn't this your day off?"

"Yes, I know, but I have to. I'll be home in less than an hour and then we can leave. Keep Emily beside you the whole time."

Her eyes are clenched up again, she's thinking about her father.

"I will. Try and rest for a little while. We're going to have a long day."

She agrees by closing her eyes and going back to sleep.

Emily is sitting up in bed, whispering into the phone when I knock softly on her door and gently push it open. She's awake early, too, talking to one of her friends. "I want to have a quick run before we leave, just around the block a couple of times. Uncle Harry and Grandpa are downstairs. I won't be long." She waves me away with the hand that isn't holding the cordless phone.

Hardly gives me the same expression that I got from Heather. His eyes are narrow little slits, and he looks like he's been awake all night. "You are mad, aren't you? Absolutely certifiable."

My dad thinks it's a good idea, though. He's in the kitchen and has opened three cans of soup. "Go on, it'll do you good. You've got a long flight ahead of you."

He turns away and I think about asking him why he's heating up soup first thing in the morning but Hardly puts his finger to his lips and shakes his head, smiling. He's right. If preparing soup makes him happy then he should heat up some soup.

Once I'm out on the sidewalk, I sprint as quickly as I can and cut through the laneway to get to her house. I don't expect her to be awake but when I'm outside the building I take a look up at the apartment with the flower pot on the balcony and see a light on. When I push the intercom button and tell her I'm here, she buzzes me in immediately. The hallways are quiet this time of morning and her door is slightly ajar. She's standing in the doorframe with her slim arms at her sides. Her hair is sticking up on one side and she looks delightfully sleepy. She gives me the look she gave me when we were children and I didn't have the nerve to talk to her.

"You're out early."

She holds her ground and doesn't move toward me or make an opening for me to enter.

"I'm leaving for a while. We're going to Canada, today, and I needed to tell you something."

She waves me into her living room and sits on the edge of the chair without inviting me to sit.

"I wanted to tell you that I have a family and my priority is…"

"I understand."

"I've enjoyed our time together but…"

"It's okay, Malcolm. I understand."

"I don't think I'll be able to run with you anymore."

She cocks her head to one side and laughs. Something doesn't feel right. I glance around the apartment as nonchalantly as I can manage. The room has no feeling. There are no photographs on the walls, no mementos of trips taken or memories cherished. It looks like a place to live but not a home. I realize there will always be much I don't know about this woman.

I don't know what else to say but when I turn to leave she begins speaking. "I lied to you. It wasn't cancer."

"Stuart?"

Her eyes are on me but it's like she isn't seeing me. "He took his father's rifle one afternoon. He drank one, single can of beer, and then he placed the barrel in his mouth and pulled the trigger."

I hear the gasp coming from my mouth and it feels as though someone else made the sound.

"He did it right in the corner of our bedroom. Left a hell of a mess for me to clean up."

I say what we all say. I tell her I'm sorry, I tell her I feel for her, but standing in her living room, a room with no soul, a little bit of me feels relieved that it wasn't me. A little bit of me is secretly glad that I don't have pains in my life that force me to pick up a gun.

She's still not really seeing me as she explains. "It wasn't his job; that was fine. Wasn't us, we had no problems, no real problems anyway. Nobody knows why he did it. He didn't even leave a note."

Her eyes finally have some life in them as she focusses on me. "I'll be okay, Malcolm. I just get lonely sometimes. Like I told you before, you take your comforts where you can."

I spent yesterday in a castle and experienced some of the history of my country and then later I stood in a graveyard where so many men and women sacrificed so much. And now I'm here. Sometimes, nothing makes sense. I start to speak. I walk toward her but she folds her arms in front of her chest. "You should go. Canada awaits you. And your girlfriend. And her daughter."

She's judging me as she says it. I don't know why or how but it feels the same way she always has. The way she might have done in the schoolyard.

I don't see or hear a thing after I close her door behind me. It's like I'm living inside my own head as I walk along the hallway and then down the stairs. When the cold air hits me outside, I breathe it in and look up at her balcony. The sun has come up. It's lighter now and I can't tell if her apartment light is on or off. I watch for a moment and then the curtains are closed. Explaining to her didn't make me feel better, but that wasn't why I did it. I don't know why she told me the truth about Stuart and I don't know why she lied either. I feel sorry for her and I hope she finds something that will take her away from the pain that she's hiding from, but it can't be me. I can't help; I can't be here. I'm glad I told her but it's only the beginning. I still need to tell Heather. It'll have to wait. This isn't the time, but I will tell her. I know what I want now.

Chapter Eighteen

BARRY ISN'T AT school yet. He's late. It's the only time I can ever remember him being late. I sit on one of the hard uncomfortable chairs outside his office as the teachers file by. None of them talk to me, but they give me their concerned looks, wondering why I'm here on my day off. I'm tired. My mind is in a hundred different places, and they can probably see it. It doesn't matter. I've never cared what they think, I've never cared what anyone thinks and I'm not going to start now. I just want to tell Barry what happened with the doctor and thank him. And I need to tell him that I'm going away for a couple of days. It's better to do that in person.

The times when the two of us come in early and sit together drinking our cups of Scottish tea before classes start are some of my favorite times. I wish we were doing that now, today. I wish that none of the other things had happened. The headmaster knows I'm not working today and asks if I can keep an eye on Barry's class until he arrives. Yes, of course, I can. I like these ones. They're excitable, just like all the kids in the school, but they're well-behaved, too. There's a hierarchy among them, like every group, but it's a positive one. They want to learn and they ask questions. I set them up with the movie that they like. I play a few minutes on the projector and then I pause it and they write down answers to questions. There are no complaints. They like it and it'll keep them busy until Barry gets here.

When the phone call comes, the secretary, Trudy, the one who can't keep her mouth shut, comes bustling into the classroom leaving the door wide open. I know it's not good. Her eyes are as wide as saucers but there's no warmth there. It feels like she's taking some kind of delight in giving me the bad news. It's like she's encouraging the disintegration of my family and she wants to see it take place right in front of everybody. She tilts her head to one side in mock sympathy when she speaks but it isn't genuine.

I stop the movie and the children all watch us. She doesn't take me into the hallway or even lead me aside and whisper in my ear to spare the children from hearing. "I'm sorry, miss, your husband, I mean, your Malcolm, has been on the telephone. It's his dad. You have to get to the infirmary."

"Alex? Something's wrong with Alex?" Two or three children have gathered in the hallway outside the classroom. I can see them through the open door, behind her. They're watching us. Their silence could peel the paint off the walls. They're eight, nine years old, full of piss and vinegar and intuitive beyond their years, but the drama quietens all of them.

"I told him you were waiting for the assistant headmaster and we were having you fill in for a little bit."

There it is. Now I know. I'm on my feet. Malcolm thinks there's something between Barry and me. I've felt it. I can tell from his questions. Now I know. She's told him. She must have spoken to him, telling him stories about how much time Barry and I spend together. Trudy, with her big hair, light blue eye-shadow, and a face that's twenty years too late.

"Miss, you need to get yourself to the infirmary."

Something has happened to Alex. I have the car. How did they get to the hospital? I'm inches from her face. "Did he not want to talk to me? Malcolm? He didn't want me to come to the phone?"

She ignores my question and purses her lips together almost sarcastically. "I'll let Barry know you were waiting for him. It'll be fine. You need to go."

And, I'm gone. No "goodbyes" to the children as I rush down the hallway, no more questions, just gone. Me, worrying about my foolish pride, instead of being concerned about Alex. I wish I'd brought the mobile phone with me so that I could call the hospital and try to reach Malcolm. I drive our car out of the school parking lot, gunning it as I pass the roundabout, fuming about the power the malicious woman has over me.

There's nothing happening between me and Barry. The invitations are there, I can tell. He's made cute little propositions but I've never responded, not really. And Malcolm has never asked but he thinks I've been with him. He wouldn't have checked my emails or looked at my phone calls. That's not Malcolm. He just thinks he knows and it's because of her.

They're in the emergency area of the hospital. Alex is on a gurney but he's sitting up and smiling. They're laughing at something he's said. Emily can see the shock on my face. She comes toward me while Malcolm and Hardly stand on either side of Alex.

"He dumped a pot of hot soup over his arm."

Alex speaks up over Emily. "Wasted it. Good cream of mushroom soup."

Emily smiles, and agrees with him. "Yes, he wasted it. His arm ballooned up and we three medical experts didn't know what to do so we had Mrs. Davidson's son…"

"From next door?"

"Yes, from next door. He gave us all a ride in his very small car and we came here."

"I'm fine. The nice lady doctor has given me a prescription for some cream and told me that Tesco has soup on sale. So I'll replace it for you."

Hardly has found a chair and pulls it toward him with his cane before sitting down. "I'll get him home and pick up his prescription. He'll be okay."

Malcolm hasn't spoken to me yet. I don't know what she told him but none of it is true. And even if it was, does it matter? It's too late anyway, isn't it? I look at him for a few seconds. When he speaks I don't know him. I don't know him anymore. "It's okay, Dad will be fine." He turns toward his father. "And don't worry about replacing the soup. It's probably best if you stay out of the soup aisle for a while." He stops smiling and turns back to me. "He insists that we still go."

Of course, we'll still go. We have to go.

Alex has his brave face on; he's enjoying the attention, bless his soul. "I have my other boy here beside me at my beck and call. I'll be fine."

Malcolm is concerned but he's okay, he trusts Hardly. "And I talked to Terry. I told him not to come; we'll be in and out in a day or so and then back home. It'll all work out."

Something's wrong. That didn't feel right. Back home doesn't sound right to me.

"He's reserved us a car. It'll be waiting at the airport in Toronto. He says that it's best for us to go right into the town and visit the city hall to check the records. In and out in no time, and then home." He looks at me and then to Emily, trying to reassure both of us.

He watches Emily's reaction while he speaks. She's okay. She has one hand on her Grandpa and she's nodding at Malcolm. I know that look. She trusts him. I remember when I had that look.

Chapter Nineteen

IT'S ONLY BEEN five years, but in my mind, Ontario became a distant memory. It's a dream that never happened. But, it did happen. Because of the events that took place five years ago I have a family. My life began all over again because of what happened here. We pass a sign telling us that Woodbine is five kilometers ahead and I feel nothing. So far it's just another town. When I was here last time I was chased across town and taken to the local police station where John Postman beat me while I was held down in a chair. Then, he kept me in a cell without being charged. Of all the places in my life I'd rather not re-visit, this is number one on my list, but I have to remember the positives that eventually came from it. As we drive further the road starts to look more familiar. I crane my neck to the side, looking for it. It doesn't make sense but I feel like I need to see it. There are memories that linger in my mind from this town, too and I need to exorcise them from my consciousness. There's no traffic so I slow down and scan the side of the highway. The motel is gone. All that's left is the base where the buildings sat. Across from where the row of rooms sat side by side, the smaller structure that faced the rooms partially remains. There was a laundry room there with a storage building beside it. There's still no other traffic so I pull over to the side of the road and look toward where the office was. I can picture the drunken manager sitting at his chair with his feet up, grinning at me, daring me. I need to get closer. I'm a hundred meters past but I swerve the car back across the empty freeway, breaking five or six traffic laws in the process.

"Malcolm." Heather is in the back seat and Emily is leaning against her, still tired from the flight and the long drive from Toronto airport. After arriving we got into the rental car and drove directly out to Woodbine. Heather has a blanket that we picked up at one of the airport shops draped over Emily as though it will protect her from all harm, real and imagined.

"I'm sorry; I just need to take a look."

I can tell that Emily is awake. She's keeping her eyes closed while her mother holds onto her, but I know she can hear us. Heather whispers anyway. "You'll wake her."

"You're right. I'll be more careful."

I pull into the parking lot. From my driver's seat I can see that the foundation of the main building still remains. There's been a recent snowfall and there is a light trace of the white powder all around us. Within the few bricks on the ground, rotted pieces of wood are jutting up. It was a fire; it had to be. The building was a community eyesore but also a temporary home for passing truckers or discreet travelers like Heather and myself when we stayed here years ago.

As I unlock the door Heather starts to speak but I cut her off. "I'll be right back."

I leave the rental car in the middle of the old motel's parking lot and jump out, wrapping my scarf around my throat and pulling my jacket tight. Heather is still holding onto Emily. The deal they made before getting on the plane was that Emily could come but Heather wasn't going to let her out of her sight.

Faded checkered white marks on the ground indicate where the parking spots were in front of the rooms. I have no trouble visualizing where ours was, directly across from the laundry room. All that remains of my hiding place is a door that's barely hanging on a doorframe and the front and side walls. I push against the door and it creaks, swinging open to a room that has no back wall. The open freeway sits behind it. There's nothing in the space, long looted and pilfered of anything that might be of value, I suppose. Even the walls have been stripped of the copper wiring as thieves and vandals must have torn the last tangible asset from the wreck. I turn back toward where the motel once stood, where my room sat when Heather's father, John Postman, broke in. I remember jogging across the yard and stealing his keys and then running terrified down the highway. I remember more, too. I remember what it felt like to lean against that wall and wait for him. I know what was going through my head. I haven't thought about those feelings for a long time. There was something about Heather, something about that girl. I wanted her. I wanted to help her even though I knew she was lying. She'd been playing me perhaps ever since our visit to the lake months before, but it didn't matter. When we were together and I held her and all the outside stuff was gone, everything worked, everything was right. I wonder what happens to those feelings. I wonder how we can discard them or forget about them so easily. Is it because of what we do or is it because of what we think our partner has done? Do rumors and innuendoes that we hear from a gossipy co-worker matter? I get back into the car and settle myself into the seat.

Now Emily really is sleeping. She's lying on the seat, half across Heather. I can hear her breathing heavy and her chest is moving up and down. She was just a child last time we were here. So much has happened since then.

I'm beginning to remember my way around the town now. I look at Heather in the back seat. "I want to go past the house, and then we'll go into town."

"I don't understand what you're doing. Why would you want to go to these places?"

I look down at Emily as I answer. "Because we can't be afraid of them and neither can Emily. They're just places. And I want to find somebody who'll confirm that he's dead. The police chief dying would have been a big deal; people must still talk about it. Maybe one of his old neighbors will talk to me." Emily stirs. She's listening now. "We can't be afraid, Heather; it's no way to live."

There can be no more ghosts in our lives. After a moment she nods her head, reluctantly agreeing.

When it was all over and we were safely ensconced in Scotland, we never investigated wills or inheritances. Somehow, it found us though. When the paperwork arrived, Terry suggested a Canadian lawyer who handled the estate. Heather was the only heir other than an uncle, a brother of her father's, whom the family hadn't kept in contact with. She didn't want anything from him and it didn't matter to us; we just wanted to be done with the man, the whole town. His house, the house where Heather grew up and where Emily lived, looks the same as it did the last time we were here. There's a "For Sale" sign on the front lawn with a "Sold" sticker plastered across it. Obviously, the resident who bought the property after the estate sold it didn't live here for too long. Across the street there's a man using a shovel to knock hanging icicles from the eaves under his garage. I pull in front of Postman's house and walk over to the elderly gentleman in as friendly a manner as I can muster.

"It sold then? Looks like you're going to have new neighbors."

That whole small-town friendliness didn't apply to Woodbine the first time I was here and it doesn't appear to be happening this time either. The man stops and leans on his shovel, staring at me, watching, but not talking.

"I noticed it for sale a couple of times but never did anything about it. Didn't the old police chief live there at one time?"

"Not my business." He leaves the shovel leaning against the garage and turns toward his house. When he reaches the door he goes in without looking back and when I look at his front window I think I see the slight flicker of the curtain as if he's off to the side watching me. Maybe it's my imagination. It was only yesterday when a woman hid behind a curtain in her apartment while I was down below, looking up. I might be wrong; it could be my mind playing tricks. As I get into the car I mentally remind myself that I probably made the correct decision when I became an accountant. Detective school would have been wasted on me.

"Malcolm, I understand what you're doing, but I don't want Emily to stay here overnight. In and out, remember?"

I drive into the center of the small town. The town hall is one of the newer buildings and looks out of place amongst the old, historic structures around it. There's less ice and snow on the main street, as though it's been cleared recently. People are walking up and down the sidewalks, oblivious to the cold. I park the car out front and we huddle up and trudge into the building. There's a row of offices along the wall, each with matching doors. Each door has the department name clearly listed in bold letters. We find the door we're looking for very quickly. Once inside, we watch as an elderly woman gives instructions to a young man while she buttons up her jacket. She smiles as she passes us on her way out. We stand at the counter with Emily between us. The man is twenty, perhaps a little older. He looks at Emily and smiles. "Somebody is tired."

Heather takes the lead. "Yes, we traveled a long way to get here." She leans forward toward him, tempting him with a smile, hoping for a response. "We're hoping you can give us some information on a death that happened in town a few years ago."

The young man ignores Emily and me. He's more interested in helping Heather with her green eyes and half-dimple. "Well, I'll certainly try. First, we need to fill out a request form."

Heather gives him her pouty face.

He's taken the bait. I know how he feels; I've been on the receiving end of that look. "It's fine, the form is simple. We'll do it together. I just need some identification."

Heather pulls her wallet from her purse and hands the man her passport as he quickly fills out the form.

"Almost all the records are up here already. Almost all of them." He sighs and wipes his forehead, indicating that he's overworked. "I've started to transition hard copies of the material to the computer but it's a laborious process." He looks over at the door where the woman left and whispers in a conspiratorial tone. "It shouldn't take this long, but it is."

Heather fills in her father's name and dates of birth and death. The man looks at the form. "It depends on whether I've transitioned it yet or not. My guess is no. I think this would still be in hard copy format." He stares at the form for a moment longer. "This name is familiar to me."

Heather's back stiffens as the man speaks. I gently place my hand on her shoulder, trying to comfort her.

The man walks backward. He's holding onto the form, but he keeps talking. Behind him in the large open area there are walls full of shelves with files and boxes spread all over the floor. Almost every open space is filled with files or boxes.

"Yes, now I remember. We had a phone call and an electronic request from a lawyer asking about this very same person."

Terry. Not a problem, it was just Terry.

"My supervisor," he points behind us toward the entrance where the woman left, "decided to ignore the requests while we migrate everything over. But since you're here in person," he whispers to us, "and she isn't here." He smiles broadly. "I'm happy to oblige."

His trained eyes scan boxes and files. He moves one from one pile and then to another. Then he goes to the wall and scans through the shelves. "There's a waiting area back there, to the left of the entrance door. This might take a few minutes."

It's Heather's turn to give him an exaggerated deep sigh. "It's fine. We'll stay right here." She's right. He's being very helpful but we don't want him getting complacent even for a moment, or deciding that the form isn't filled out correctly. And we certainly don't want his supervisor returning.

It feels as though he has no idea where anything is. It must show on our faces. He's quick to correct us. "I've been through this stuff over and over. Believe me, there is a system here. I'll find your deceased."

And he does. After a few minutes, with clinical precision he pulls a thin file from a box and marches over to us. "There's a forty-five dollar charge and then I'll be happy to make you a copy of the death certificate if you like."

I pull out my wallet and Heather opens her purse at the same time. We have sterling pounds, British money, but no Canadian dollars. We didn't have time. We stopped to eat earlier but we paid with a credit card.

I know the answer before I ask. "Will you take a credit card?"

"I'm sorry but I can't."

Heather puts sixty British pounds on the counter and looks at me. I square myself up to the young man. "Do you know the current exchange rate?" He's a nerdy, computer guy; he must know that the pound is valued higher than the dollar.

He stops looking at Heather's beckoning face for a moment and gives me a forced smile. "Not precisely but I know that's too much."

"You're right but it's all I have. Donate the balance to charity or do whatever you like with it but we really do need a copy of that certificate." I try to be slightly menacing as I lean forward toward him. This is our moment. This is the proof that we need to appease Heather's mind and it's right in front of us.

Heather gently puts her hand on my chest.

His face squirms but he doesn't move. Maybe it's the oddness of my Scottish accent or maybe because I'm getting in between him and Heather but he isn't budging.

It takes Heather and her green eyes one more try. "Please, it's really important."

Emily is watching everything, standing between us. I get the impression that she'd like to rip the file out of his hands. In about ten seconds if she doesn't do it, I will.

"I'll be right back."

Either he's calling the police or he's doing the right thing. Heather keeps staring straight ahead but Emily looks up at me. It takes two minutes before he comes back with a copy of the certificate. Heather takes it from him and reads it while I thank the man and push the money across the counter.

She holds it in front of the three of us. It takes a moment for the words to make sense to me. It says what we knew. John Postman is dead. Cause of death was a motor vehicle accident. There are no ghosts. The date matches. It's him.

The man has stepped back from the counter and is watching us. Emily is in the middle and the three of us are so close it's as though we're joined together. All of us exhale at the same time as we read the certificate. We still haven't moved when Heather asks, "Is there anything else in that folder?"

He's seen it from the expressions on our faces. He knows how important it is now. He holds the folder upside down, showing us that it's empty. He speaks quietly. "No, nothing else. All we have is the death certificate."

"But, this doesn't say where he was buried."

"They never do but if he was a resident then it would be at Polson."

"Yes, of course, I should have known that. Thank you."

I thank him, too. When we're at the door he calls out. "You don't have to leave this money. It's okay." We're gone though and I don't want it back.

When we're in the car, the two of them sit in the back seat again. They're staring at the certificate. After a moment Heather looks up at me. "I need to see him still."

"I know that. Tell me where I'm going."

"It's Polson Cemetery. I've been there before. I know where it is."

Emily hasn't said anything in a while. "Another graveyard."

I turn toward her. "I'm sorry honey, yes, another graveyard."

I pull into a parking spot across the street and back onto the road that takes us in the direction we just came from. In my rearview mirror, I can see the police station, and I remember what happened there. A shiver runs up my spine and it startles me. I need to remind myself of what I've told Heather and Emily. We can't be afraid of things. It's just a building, just another town. And, now we have definite proof. There are no ghosts.

Chapter Twenty

FROM TIME TO time she tells me where to turn as the two of them continue looking at the certificate. Could it be this easy? A crusty old town clerk didn't want to give out information on the phone as she resisted the inevitable upgrading of the town's records onto a computer disc? And Terry was too focused on land transfers to pull the information out of them. I suppose sometimes mysteries can have simple answers.

It's all coming back and I recognize more of the terrain. Woodbine is a sparsely populated town but it's spread out over a fairly large area so it's true that it is indeed a small town, but it's false also. There are large parcels of land spread out between the areas where people live, the farms, and the small commercial area of the town, so the surrounding area seems to go on for miles. I'm driving slowly, listening to her, but it feels as though we're going in circles.

"I'm getting confused. I know it's out here. I've been here. They don't move cemeteries do they?"

She doesn't want to ask Emily if she remembers where it might be. She was ten years old; it's probably not a destination that she was familiar with and it's best not to ask her. Heather is stroking Emily's hair while she's talking to me. She's doing it for Emily but she's trying to keep herself calm, too.

Emily sits up straight. "We need to ask somebody. I don't really want to see any more of this place." I've never heard her sound so firm.

Heather puts the palms of her hands in the air, submitting, agreeing.

I know what to do. "I remember this area a little bit. There's a bar back there. Let's go back and I'll go in and ask."

Heather starts to speak but it's my turn to cut her off. "I'll be fine. This isn't Dodge City. It'll be different from last time. And somebody there should be able to confirm what you have in your hands and tell us where the cemetery is. Bars are always full of story-tellers."

I find it quite easily. The bar is in the industrial area of town, past welding shops and Quonset huts full of working people. To appease Heather, I lock the doors and have the two of them sit in the front seats with the vehicle facing outward and the motor running. They'll be fine and I'll only be a minute or two.

I was here once before but it's changed. It looks as though it's had a bit of a renovation. There are no more dark corners. Somehow it's been brightened up, and it seems as though it's jumped ahead a couple of decades. The sound of an old Canadian rock band is playing from overhead speakers. There's a pool table with a man standing on either side holding a cue. When the balls hit each other on the table, friendly barbs are traded back and forth. It's different now. I don't have the same fear I had when I was here last time. If anybody is going to be able to answer questions, it's going to be somebody sitting in a bar, and I want more than just directions. I want to know if anybody remembers a policeman who was killed in a road accident on a snowy night five years ago. This is the place where somebody might remember.

The bartender is a young, fresh-faced boy who looks out of place. Even though there are only a few people sitting, drinking at tables and the two men standing around the pool table, he puts his arms in the air submissively, feigning that he's busy, and asks me to wait. I turn around and watch as one of the men methodically hits ball after ball into the corner pockets as his friend good-naturedly accuses him of cheating. A waitress appears through the door behind the counter and whispers to the barman. He swears in frustration. A couple of men dressed in greasy overalls come in at the same time and he calls to them as he makes his way into the back room, following the waitress.

"I'll be right with you guys. Give me a minute."

They barely acknowledge him as he goes back to sort out whatever business the waitress talked to him about. I scan their faces, hoping to find an expression that looks friendly enough, someone that might answer a few questions, but they're engrossed in a conversation with each other. I can hear the barman chasing someone off at the back of the pub, a panhandler I suppose or someone who's been barred. Then I hear the voice. It's impossible, but it's him. I know it is. I remember it from the last time I was here - that unmistakable French accent.

I take off out the front door and pass Heather and Emily sitting in our car. I wave at their surprised expressions, motioning that I'm okay, and I keep walking fast. By the time I reach the side door of the pub, the confrontation with the barman is over. Claude is shuffling away, hunched over. His back is to me but I know it's him. I call his name but he doesn't break stride. He just keeps moving away from me. He's wearing a long tattered jacket and the seams at the side are split open. When I get up beside him I can see that his hair is long and matted and he has a patchy beard on his face as though the hair has been cut off in clumps. He's muttering to himself, in his own private world. His left arm, closest to me, tenses up, ready for whatever aggravation I might offer him and his eyes dart quickly from side to side, violently appraising me. He walks a little faster. His muttering voice is obscenity-laden and each sentence ends with a question. It's difficult to say whether it's English or French. It's like he's speaking some other language known only to him. I was right, though. It was his voice. It's definitely him.

131

I put my hand on his shoulder as gently as I can and he spins away from me. We're facing each other and he pulls a short iron pipe from the pocket of his tattered jacket. He looks at me threateningly, eyes afire below the unruly, greasy hair that's falling onto his face. When he speaks, it's English this time.

"Wallet, money. Now."

Same old story. He's trying to take my money, just like last time.

"Claude…"

He steps back half a step and swings the pipe in front of himself. His face is caked with dirt, the kind of dirt that comes from sleeping rough for a long, long time. He doesn't know me. I know he doesn't.

"Wallet, asshole."

I take out my wallet and pull a twenty-pound note out. Then I take another one and I place my wallet back in my pocket while our eyes stay locked on each other. I fold the bills up and pass them to him. He doesn't seem to recognize that it's a foreign currency. He swipes it away immediately.

"Claude. Wait. It's me. It's Malcolm, Mr. Malcolm. Don't you remember me?"

He puts my money into the inside pocket of his long overcoat, the pipe still firmly held in his other hand. He still shows no sign of recognition. He starts to back away but I follow him, keeping pace. Heather's here. She pulls the car up alongside us. She must see what's happening. She stops suddenly and honks the horn. He looks for just an instant and I lunge and grab the pipe away from him and throw it to the curb behind me. His eyes are large now, full of panic as he backs away.

Now he knows. He does remember. "Yeah, I know who you are. You started it all. You started it. You made her leave."

There's peripheral damage in every situation and there certainly must have been when we left Woodbine. Claude was the odd man out. Postman is dead. Thank god for that. We know he is; we have proof now. But somehow Claude must have got caught in the crossfire.

"Who left, Claude? Heather? Emily? They had to get out of here."

We stop walking and he smiles.

"My wife, Scottish man, my wife left. You started all this shit with your questions and your police. I told you when you got here. I don't do police and you shouldn't have either."

"Claude, you remember, the cop, the captain..."

He shakes a little as he speaks. "I know him. I see him at the gates of hell."

With his French/English accent and liberal use of tenses, I can't tell if he's saying he still sees Postman or he saw him once. He's less intimidating now and he looks smaller than when we first met. I feel sorry for him. This can't just be a coincidence. I need to ask him. He'll know. "Come on. I have a car over here. We'll get you something to eat."

I turn toward the car and when he hasn't moved I call back over my shoulder. "Come on, it's okay. You can keep the money. I'll buy you some food."

Heather has the window down. "Malcolm, is it you that does this? Do you attract trouble in this place? Please, let's just go."

"It's Claude, the guy from the motel. He was here, at the back of the pub. Heather, there's a reason we bumped into him; there has to be. I have to help him."

"I don't remember him. Does he know where the cemetery is?"

I look over at him. He's holding the notes I gave him in his hand now and looking at me with a curious expression.

"Yeah, I'll bet he does. I owe him this, Heather. I want to get him some food. I think there's a diner..."

"Yes, I know where that is." She's been watching him over my shoulder. She might not remember who he is but it's difficult to turn away from someone who's in a state like he is. "You can take him in for food but we're staying in the car." As I turn away she continues, whispering this time. "And I'm opening all the windows when he gets in."

He doesn't remember her and barely acknowledges the two of them as he warily lifts himself into the back seat beside me. Heather and Emily both say hello but he doesn't answer. She's turned the heat to maximum to warm us up while the windows are down to try and expunge the odor coming from our passenger.

We settle into a booth in the diner while Heather and Emily wait in the car. The swagger that I remember is gone. From time to time it re-emerges in a look or a flip remark but the bold cockiness that surrounded his every move is no longer with him. He smells of liquor just like he always did but now it's permeated into him along with the odor of stale cigarettes and too many nights spent sleeping outside. The waitress shakes her head firmly from side to side when she sees him but when I tell her that he's with me and ask her to bring him one of their daily specials, she reluctantly nods and turns around.

His skin is weather-hardened but his eyes are alert, darting around the restaurant every time somebody moves.

"What do you do, Claude? How do you survive?"

He laughs a short, throaty laugh and is about to make a smart remark. Half of his mouth curls and I wait in anticipation for it but then he seems to change his mind.

"I get by. My old lady lives with a logger not too far from here. She feeds me sometimes and I get help here and there."

The waitress plops a plate of Salisbury steak and mashed potatoes in front of him but keeps her head aloft as though she's trying to avoid his odor. He doesn't care. He gives her the smile that he's probably been using on women since he was a teenager. It's too late, though. It's not going to work, and she quickly walks away.

He slops back a few spoonfuls of potatoes and munches on the gravy-covered steak and before I know it his plate is almost empty. He starts speaking as he eats the last few bites, being careful that not even a morsel escapes from his mouth.

"It burned down. The motel, the storage sheds, everything. Nobody was there when it started. They'd all cleared out except me. Insurance job for sure but nothing, and I mean nothing, to do with me. That doesn't mean jack of course, so I get banged up in a nine by nine while the cops try to beat it out of me. There was nothing to tell, though. I woke up and felt the heat. Never mind seeing the flames bouncing off the roof, I feel the heat even from my place."

I believe him. I'm not sure why but I think he's telling the truth.

"When I got out of the jailhouse Lise had left with the milkman."

"I thought she lived with a logger."

"Milkman first then logger later. Milkman couldn't deliver if you know what I mean."

I have no choice. I laugh at the absurdity of it all and after a moment he softens up and laughs with me.

"What happened to your woman? Did you find her?"

"That's her in the car."

He nods, as though he just remembered that he'd had a ride in our car. "Yes, in the car."

"We live in Scotland now with her daughter, our daughter."

He nods again, accepting. "That's good. The cop died and everybody is happy. Everybody except Claude."

I reach out and touch his arm. He tenses up, expecting a challenge.

"How do you know he died?"

"Everybody knows he died. Boss-man cop dies in snowstorm. One night he tears apart your room looking for you. Then the next night he gets killed on the highway. It happens. Roads are treacherous. I see lots."

He shakes my hand free and sucks on his hot coffee, slurping it up.

"You've never seen him again? He never shook you up in the middle of the night or looked in on you when you were in prison? I mean, how do you know? Do you really know?"

He shakes his head, regarding me as though I've just flown in from another planet.

"This shit again. Crazy-eyes cop, the head cop is dead. I know these things. I told you when we first met. I don't do cops, never have. You just don't get it."

I nod my head, satisfied. "Good, good. That's what I thought. I thought he died."

The food is finished and his plate is clean. The waitress has refilled his cup and he hurriedly drinks it. I know him. There's only one thing left. I pull out my wallet and give him the last two bills I have. I know what he's going to do with the money but I don't care.

"Take these to the bank. They'll change them into dollars for you."

He's figured it out now. "You here long?"

"I don't think so. I think we've found out enough. We need to find the cemetery now. Do you know where it is?"

"Of course." He waits. The only thing missing is his hand being held out.

"Claude, I have no money left. Just tell me."

He gives me a heavy sigh. "You're close to it from here." He points out the window and reels off some simple directions. We were almost there earlier. We must have almost driven past it. Heather was right; we were in the correct area.

"Thank you. Can we drop you somewhere? We're going to head to the cemetery and then maybe to the police station after we're done."

When I say the magic word, he's up from his chair and off toward the door, tucking my money into his pockets.

"Crazy, crazy, still crazy." The other diners look up from their plates as he passes, and no one seems to relax until the door has closed behind him. I watch him walking to the side of the highway, looking over his shoulder behind himself every few steps. When there's a break in the traffic he half-runs across. When he gets to the other side he keeps walking fast. He looks back one last time before I lose sight of him, and then he's gone.

Chapter Twenty-One

SOMETHING FEELS DIFFERENT. *I don't know if it happened when we left the town hall or when I held the certificate in my hand and saw those words, but I feel okay. I feel like I'm going to be okay. There are a lady and a man standing beside Malcolm, doing their best to help him. Emily is glued to Malcolm's side, and the man and woman are pointing and showing them where we need to go. I lock the car and catch up to them. Emily is still close to Malcolm. We spoke in the car, and she's okay. She doesn't want to be here anymore. But she's okay.*

"It's further down; the lady said it should be in the middle of the row." Malcolm is leading the way.

"I can't believe I'm in my second cemetery in a week. I'd never been in one before. The gravestone-thingys are smaller here." She's shaking her head.

She's never been here so that means he never brought her. He never showed her.

It's here. I suck in a deep breath. He's here. Of course, he is. It's a small flat stone, slightly raised at the back. It has his birth and death dates and his full name. There are no other inscriptions. No mention of who he left behind, or terrorized, or tried to kill. Just a life terminated, my father, John Postman.

I take some long, deep breaths. I don't want to stand too close. I feel like something will happen if I'm closer, over beside him. It's not fear, it's just a wariness. Emily notices it first and pokes Malcolm in the side. The stone beside his is my mother's. I knew it was here. I remember coming here now. If Emily has never been here then she's never seen it.

I don't want my mother buried beside him but I have no choice and I suppose in the end it really doesn't matter. I move over and touch her stone; I was a child when she died, but I remember her a little bit. She was a good woman but she was weak and unpredictable, and moody. I wonder if she had what I have. I wonder if she was bipolar. Is it genetic, can it be handed down? Should Emily be checked for it, too?

It's cold and they want to go. They're watching me, waiting. I should say something to Emily about my mother, her grandmother, but this isn't the time. Malcolm is right, it's just a place and we can't be afraid of it. If we need to come back one day, then we'll come back.

Emily has a variation of one of her bored teenager expressions on her face. She's better now; she's coming back to us. Malcolm looks tired, though, very tired. "Yes, I'm convinced. Let's go."

As we walk back to the car, Malcolm tries to take my hand, but I can't do it. He's trying so hard. This has been difficult for him, too. He had to face down the man who he left to die. This wasn't easy for him either. There are some days when I love him and other days when I'm not so sure. I don't think it should be like that. Should there be other people? I don't ask him who he's with when he's out running at odd hours and even though he thinks something happened with Barry he's wrong. We never did anything.

I speak slowly, loud enough for both of them to hear. "I'm sorry."

"There's no need. I'm glad we came. Now we know."

An unusual sensation comes over me. I feel like I'm in a daze. Malcolm and Emily are beside me but they're not really here. It's like an epiphany. In the middle of a graveyard in my country, my home country, it comes to me. I don't hate my father anymore. It doesn't come as a shock; it's just there, and I know it's true. I can feel it. I don't feel happy about it, but maybe I never have been. Was I ever a happy person, even as a child? Do I know how to find happy? The feelings keep coming. Malcolm sees it and tries to hold me but I pull away from him. He won't understand. It's not satisfaction or remorse, it's something else. I have an idea. I know what I need to do now. I don't know why I didn't realize this before. I know what I need to do to feel better.

Emily jumps in the front seat this time and I let her. Malcolm holds the back door open and waits until I get in. He's lost, looking at me as though he's done something wrong. He'll be okay. I know he will. I pull the blanket around myself as I sit down in the back seat. Malcolm looks back and leans over, still concerned. "Airport or is there anywhere else you want to go? Claude confirmed. In fact, he thought I was nuts to doubt it."

We'd talked about going to the police station to see the officer who worked with my father. It doesn't matter now, though; we know he's dead.

"I need to go somewhere and think. Can we do that?"

The two of them look at me curiously. Emily speaks. "Mom, I want to go home."

There's one last item of unresolved business. "Malcolm, I want to find out about the holdings while we're here. My uncle is in Toronto, or he was when we did the paperwork from the estate. I want to know about the other land Terry was talking about. Can we call him?"

He wants to get out of Woodbine, too. He answers right away. "That's a good idea. I'll head us toward Toronto and you two can call Terry from the mobile and see if he's found anything else out. We may as well make use of his expensive toy."

Emily's face is down and she looks tired. "Em, then we'll get out of here. I promise."

After a misdial and dropping the call, Emily gets Terry on the phone and puts him on speaker, laying it on the console beside her. Malcolm fills him in on the details and confirms that we found the grave. I can tell that Jo, in her intuitive way, has figured out how important this trip was. She must have explained to Terry the gravity of it all because he's speaking slowly and more carefully now.

"I'm glad. I hope, well I just hope you all got what you needed while you were there. I will also mention that I've checked flights and the three of you could be here by tomorrow morning. We'd love to welcome you to the west coast."

Emily lets out a groan. Terry and she have never met but they've got to know each other by communicating over the computer while Malcolm visits with his friend.

"I heard that, young lady."

"Sorry, sorry, sorry."

Malcolm explains. "She just wants to get home, buddy. It's been a tough couple of days."

"I know. You're off the hook, Emily, no worries. Maybe we'll see you in the summer."

We pass the sign telling us we're leaving Woodbine. The three of us watch it as the car leaves the town in the distance, and Malcolm turns us onto the main highway. There's a little traffic but it's moving quickly. Cars move on either side of us. Everything is the same and everything is different. My father is dead. I know now for sure that he died.

I pipe up from the backseat. "Terry, my uncle, the Charles Postman you mentioned, I never met him, but I know he's quite a bit older than me. He and his wife are in Toronto which is only a few hours from us now. I've never been to his place but I was wondering..."

"I wondered the same thing, Heather. I didn't know how old he was either because we dealt with his lawyer last time, but I wanted to know more about him in regards to the land dealings, so I took the liberty, I hope you don't mind."

He did what he likes to do. Part of his success is due to his curiosity. I remember that from when I worked for him. "No, I'm glad you did. Please tell us everything you found out."

"Okay, buckle up you guys because this is going to blow your mind."

Malcolm keeps his eyes on the road but Emily has turned toward the phone and has her hands on her knees, waiting for the story to begin.

"Charles Postman was predeceased by his wife two years ago. This was a second wife. They married only four years ago, so chances are you did not know her Heather."

He's right; I heard very little about him when I was growing up.

"Charles is ninety this year. Now we used the same lawyer that helped us initially with the estate. Remember I had him liaising with your uncle and the lawyer in Ontario, and we couriered the documents back and forth."

I don't. I remember very little about that time except I wanted it all to go away. I took a little bit of money from the estate and Malcolm and I used it to help buy our house. The rest I didn't want. I just wanted to move on.

"Well, I had my lawyer contact him again, directly this time, not through his lawyer. He was actually quite happy to hear from us. I couldn't tell him that we

were acting on your behalf, because really we weren't. So he told him that it was a follow-up to the paperwork that had been done when the estate was transferred to him. That was mostly true but he's quite an astute fellow, this Charles Postman, even at his age, and I'm pretty sure he knew that you were on the other side of this thing."

"Terry, I don't know much about him. He didn't have children so there was no connection there and even if he did they'd be older than me. I do seem to remember being told that he had gone off on his own. I think he lived in Woodbine at one point but something happened and he left. That was long before I was born, though."

There's a slight pause before Terry answers again. "I don't have that information. I was more interested in the assets from the estate and the land transfers that have been happening. He did confirm what we knew already. You signed over the bulk of the assets."

It's coming back to me now. "I signed over all of them Terry."

"Heather, remember when we dealt with this we were going in blind. We didn't know what John Postman owned or had acquired. We did the best we could but it was difficult. Your uncle discovered other assets and that's the land that I found out about when I did the research. Charles placed that land in a blind trust and the rest of the assets from the estate he sold. They were all converted to cash."

"So that explains it. There was no one else selling land, it was all Charles."

There's silence on the other end of the line.

Malcolm speaks up without looking away from the road. "Terry, have we lost you? Can you confirm that no one else was involved?

"Sorry guys, Jo was saying something to me. Yes, no one else was involved, it was all Charles. He sold the land and the assets, all of it, and he's forwarded the funds to my lawyer out here."

Malcolm screws up his face. "Why to you, Terry."

Jo has been listening, too. She speaks up. "He wants all the money to be paid to Heather, Malcolm."

Terry jumps back in. "And the deeds to the land in the blind trust. That's yours, too, Heather. He doesn't want it. None of it."

I answer quickly. "We don't really need money, though. And I don't know if I want it."

Jo jumps in again. "Heather and Malcolm and Emily, sorry, hello, it's Jo here. You need to think of this money as coming from Charles, your uncle. He's an old man who probably doesn't have much time left. It's his money, and he wants you to have it. That's it. Nothing else."

She's right. And we should have it.

I'm sure we're all thinking the same thing but none of us will ask. I know Terry, though. He wants to tell us. It'll be eating at him.

"Cash is just under eight hundred thousand. That's Canadian dollars folks, not sterling. And current market value of the land is four million dollars. Again, that's Canadian funds."

There's silence in the car, and from the phone.

Terry again. "You guys just became very wealthy. Congratulations."

Malcolm pulls the car off the road, over to the side of the highway, and speaks toward the phone. "Terry, we really appreciate you doing all this. We're going to need some time to process."

Terry and Jo at the same time now. "Of course you do, of course you do."

"Terry, before you go, should we go and see Charles?"

"He doesn't want any contact, Heather. I would leave it. He was quite content to have the whole business behind him. He was quite cordial with us but he's done. I wouldn't do it."

Malcolm leans toward the phone and speaks again. "Terry we'll call you when we get home. Thank you, to both of you."

"For you, for all of you, I do it. I'm glad we could help."

Jo calls goodbye over his voice and the line goes dead.

We're comfortable. We don't need anything, but this amount of money takes us to a different place. I need to sleep and I need to think. I need this information to reconcile with the idea I had earlier because this will help. It's all starting to make sense. It wasn't a coincidence that Malcolm bumped into the man from the motel and this isn't a coincidence either. It happened for a reason. When I think about what I want to do it makes me feel calm, and it might not be as crazy as I think it is. I'm feeling better and it's not because of the money and it's not entirely because I now know he's dead. I won't tell Emily and Malcolm what I'm thinking. I'll wait. It's a gamble, a big one. I'm gambling with Emily but I have to do it. I'll tell them my plan once I have a chance to formulate it all.

Malcolm rubs his hand over Emily's hair. "Let's get to Toronto. We'll book into the hotel that's attached to the airport, get some rest, have a good shower in the morning and then we'll head home."

Emily adds, "I want to call Uncle Harry and see how Grandpa is doing."

We have millions of dollars coming to us but I'm the only one who has noticed.

Malcolm smiles at her. "You know Grandpa can talk to you. It's his arm that got burnt not his tongue. He can still speak."

"Yeah, and he'll tell me he's fine. But Uncle Harry will tell me everything." She waits for a moment and then repeats it. "Everything."

Malcolm laughs as Emily nods in her young, knowing way. "Sounds good: hotel, a phone call to Uncle Harry, and home by tomorrow."

I pull the blanket up over me and agree with them. From time to time I wake up and glance over at Emily. She's either whispering to Malcolm or staring out the window. She's okay. She got through this. Malcolm is tired. I can see the strain under his eyes in the rear-view mirror. We have millions of dollars and I know what I want to do now. I know what I need to do.

Chapter Twenty-Two

CANADA IS SKY, so much sky. The west coast, where I lived as a young man has mountains and they interrupt the sky, and Scotland has its own unique character with its hills and mountains and rough terrain. Woodbine, Ontario and the area around it is different though. The sky is much more prominent here. As we drive toward the city all I see are monotonous miles of road and the imposing sky looming in front of us. After a while we leave the countryside and reach larger towns. My two passengers are asleep and although I want to pull over and close my eyes for a few minutes I keep going. In the early hours of the morning I finally see the lights of Toronto and it feels like we've traveled into a different country. I drive us to the airport hotel and we immediately check into a room and jump into our beds. Heather sleeps with Emily and I crawl into the other one by myself. We're side by side with a night table in between. I sleep soundly but I dream the most vivid dreams. In my dreams I'm wandering through an empty graveyard. I'm alone this time, and when I turn to find Emily or Heather, or Hardly and my dad all I see is sky, heavy sky, weighing down on me. No matter which way I turn I'm by myself, alone, and the sky is empty and cold.

In the morning Heather is up first. I hear the shower running and when I pry my eyes open I see her quietly getting dressed, gently taking her clothes out of our bag, and slipping them on.

"I'll see you in a little while. Sleep, you must be exhausted."

I don't answer. I just roll over and go back to sleep. She's right; it's caught up to me, and I don't think I've ever been this tired. There's a separate room in the suite and when I wake up again I see Emily through the dividing door, sitting at the writing table, staring out the long windows that run down the wall. She calls over. "We're a long way up. It's like being up in the air. I didn't realize how high we were last night."

I laugh at her and realize that's probably what caused my dreams. I must have looked out the big windows before drifting off to sleep. "Yeah, those windows gave me really weird dreams last night. Doesn't matter, though, we could have been in outer space and I think all of us would still have slept."

"Where's Mom?"

I look at the clock on the bedside table. "She left a while back. She must be in the lobby. I'll get dressed and we'll go find her. She'll be okay. It's good that she has some time to herself."

By the time I come out into the outer room ready to go, Emily has her bag packed and is sitting at the door. "Mom called from downstairs. She's had breakfast but will sit with us while we eat. I don't know where she's getting the energy from."

"Did you ask her about...?"

"Yes, I asked her if she checked flight times but she didn't really answer."

The elevator drops us fast like a rock through the air and Emily giggles and comes over and holds onto me. When we spot Heather sitting on a large chair in the lounge she looks fresher than she should. She hugs each of us individually and then grabs both of us together, holding on for a moment. This has done it. It's helped her; she's in a good space now.

Emily talks quickly, making plans. "I looked at the book in the room. We can reserve our flight home directly from here at the hotel and there's a buffet where we can eat." She looks at her mother suspiciously. "Which you have found already. I say we head to the reservation desk, which is where we book our seats according to the information I found, and then we get some food. I'm starving." She looks over at me. "I can never figure out the time change. Is it possible for us to be home by dinner time? Or, will it be tomorrow morning?"

I'm about to answer but something isn't right. Heather hasn't moved. She's still leaning back in the chair. When she speaks her voice is calm and measured.

"I want to tell you something first, and I want to tell you both together because we've been through all of this together. I've put us through all this."

It's serious. I can tell.

"I went to a doctor before we left, and I know what's wrong with me."

I lean forward but she waves me back.

"No, I'm fine. Well, I mean I'm okay now. I haven't had confirmation yet but the doctor, who's a specialist, thinks I may have bipolar disorder."

She stops us again before we can interject. "And it's fine. He says it's treatable with medication. It'll help me to start feeling better, more balanced."

This is a good thing. I should have been there to see the doctor with her, but I'm glad she got some answers.

Emily has questions. "I'm not entirely sure I know what that means."

Heather laughs a quick, nervous laugh. "I'm not either but I know that once a problem has been identified, it can be resolved. I'm looking forward to resolving mine." She reaches out and touches Emily's hand. "And we'll learn about it together."

I'm proud of her. "That was a brave thing for you to do. I'm glad, honey."

Emily isn't convinced yet. "What do they do to you when you're bipolar? Is that why you've been hearing things?"

Heather sighs. She didn't anticipate that question. I can tell. "They treat it with medication, I think. I have a friend who is affected by it and he takes pills that make him feel better." She looks at me now. "And no, I don't know if what I heard had anything to do with this. I'll have to ask the doctor." She pauses, still leaning back in her chair. "Maybe there was nothing there. We know now, so maybe it was my imagination. I don't know."

Emily smiles at her mother. "I'm glad, Mom. I'm glad you're going to feel better, and I'll read about it, but I really want to eat and then check out flights. Can we talk more about it on the plane?"

We're sitting in a small circle in three plush, comfortable lounge chairs all facing each other. Heather leans back. She isn't finished yet. She's gathering her courage. She takes a deep breath and falters, then after a moment, she continues. "There's something else. I'm sorry, Malcolm." She looks at me and then down for a moment. I have a sick feeling in my stomach. "I've decided that I'm not going back to Scotland. I need to sort some things out. The doctor helped me with some of this but since we've been here I've made a decision. I'm not going back."

At first I think that I've misheard her. I replay her words in my head and watch her expression closely and then I realize. I should have known. I should have seen this coming. I feel like I'm back in my dream again with nobody beside me. I don't know what to say. She's not choosing a country; she's choosing to not be with me.

Emily is angry. She leans toward her mother, but Heather keeps speaking.

"I need some time to sort things out and I know that won't happen in Scotland."

Emily wants answers. "Where are you thinking of going? Do you need a holiday?"

Heather finds some courage. She looks at me. "No, this won't be a holiday. I, we're," She looks at Emily, "going to stay here. Well, not here, but in Canada. You and I are going back to the west coast."

She looks from Emily to me and then back again, waiting. I'm on my feet but I don't know how I stood up. I'm not sure what to do. I want to tell her that she can't. We've slain the dragon and now everything will be okay. I want to tell her that we've made it, but when I look at her face I know it isn't true.

She's up now, too. She holds me tight and whispers in my ear, quietly so Emily can't hear. "I love you. I just don't think I'm in love with you."

When she lets go I can tell from her eyes that it isn't there anymore. Maybe it hasn't been there in a long time.

Emily is shaking her head. "How can you just? Is it the bipolar? I don't understand."

"No, it's not. I need to make this change. I have some things I want to do. I have no purpose in Scotland. I need to do something with my life. I don't want to keep feeling unfulfilled. It isn't worth it."

Emily stares at her mother as though she's a stranger.

Heather keeps speaking. "Em, we'll start over in Canada again. You'll love the west coast. B.C. is so beautiful and we won't be alone. Terry and Jo are there."

"But we will be alone."

I breathe in and breathe out, waiting.

Heather keeps watching her daughter. "Yes, it'll be just you and me."

It's quiet. It's so quiet. The time stretches and hangs; it's suffocating me. Is this how it was for my father when my mother left him?

Emily stands up and looks at her mother. She's definite when she answers. "I'll be going home. To Scotland. If that's okay with you, Dad."

I look at Heather and she is smiling a brave smile, not agreeing or disagreeing. Tears roll down her cheeks. She must have known that this might happen. She must have thought about it. She sits back down. Nobody speaks and then she wipes her tears away and nods at me, trying to smile.

Emily is crying now, too but she's decided. She looks at me and says the saddest thing I've ever heard. "I'll go to school in Scotland and visit my mother in the summer. It'll give her time to settle and figure things out."

She's looking at me for confirmation for acceptance, for anything. There's only one answer. I've lost one of them. I'm not going to lose both of them. I sit back in the chair and hold tight to the armrests. I take a deep breath and answer her right away.

Chapter Twenty-Three

Five Years Later

I HOLD ONTO his thick, calloused hand. It's become softer as he's aged. The machine mounted to the wall above the bed beeps periodically and he takes little breaths. The breaths come out in little tufts, just barely escaping from his lips.

I keep talking. I don't want to acknowledge that it's real, that I'm here, so I just keep talking. "And I'm good. Emily is here, too."

I motion over toward her. She's on the other side of the bed, holding onto his other hand. She can't see because of her tears. She tries to focus and then gives up, just looking in his general direction, blinking her eyes from time to time.

I keep going because I'm afraid of what might happen if I stop. "She's going to be smarter than all of us, Dad. She wants to be a historian. Can you imagine that – we're going to have a historian in the family?"

Emily puts her head down on her grandfather. As her face hits his chest, there's a slight reaction from him and part of me believes. I believe he'll wake up and he'll be okay, and we'll be back at his house by nighttime, eating tomato soup and talking about fitba games.

The little tufts of air continue. They're less frequent now. I'm running out of time. "And we're doing fine, Dad. We're all happy.

I'm happy." I sob. I don't know where it comes from but it's there. I let out a sob of regret, happiness, confusion – everything all at the same time. "It's true Dad. We're all good."

The door opens and Hardly is here. Gerald "Hardly" McDougall, my friend, my brother, my father's surrogate son, rushes to the side of the bed and stands in front of me.

"I thought I wouldn't make it. Flora is parking the car. When we were here last night he seemed okay." He looks down at our father, and thankfully the little tufts of air keep coming out.

When we returned from Ontario, Emily and me, our lives fell into a pattern. She recovered from her mother's absence surprisingly quickly. For a while, she talked about how her mom might come back to us but I couldn't let myself believe that and I don't think she really did either. She just said it to try and make me feel better. When Heather spoke to us at the airport in Toronto she'd made her decision. I could tell. She wasn't just leaving Scotland; she was leaving me, too.

You think you have a forever plan and then somebody says you're on the wrong page and the plan wasn't yours to begin with. So you do what you have to do in order to survive. You find a song that means something and you play it loud, and it helps you forget for a few minutes. You breathe in and you breathe out and the feeling passes for a while. Sometimes it's a minute and then it becomes an hour and before you know it the hours turn into days. And then one day you find yourself out running, or you're helping your father, or you're planning a trip with your daughter to visit an old battleground that she has to study for a school project, and it's gone. Before you know it a year has passed and you're different and you think that nobody has noticed. They do, though. The ones close to you know that it's changed you a little bit. We survived; we survived all of it. Emily surrounded herself with her friends and her studies and I held on to the same people I've always held on to.

Emily sat me down after a year and had a talk with me. There was a boy, Michael. He'd been studying with her, sitting at our kitchen table giggling and talking about the battle of Culloden He'd been thoroughly vetted by her grandfather and her uncle Harry by the time I met him. They knew his family, right down to which street where his parents had lived on when they were growing up as children themselves. I liked him. He and Emily had a shared love of history and he made her laugh. She waited until Michael left and then she beckoned me to the table.

"You need to meet someone."

When I start to speak she cuts me off. "I have no problem with it, so don't worry about me. I think it would be good for you."

I smile and try not to laugh.

She has a serious expression on her face but she's having difficulty maintaining it. "I just want you to be happy. You're a catch."

"Em, I appreciate that you're giving me this opportunity."

"I'm going to hit you."

"I mean it. I really do. Now, which of your teachers are single?"

For a moment she thinks I'm serious. "No, that's too close to me. You need to find someone away from my school."

When the laughter escapes from my mouth, she reaches across the table and slaps me on the chest the same way she used to slap her grandfather when she was a little girl.

"I'm just saying."

"And, I appreciate it."

I didn't do it. I needed to wait longer. For a while there was the occasional brief moment of weakness when my thoughts went backward, and I allowed myself to believe that the green-eyed girl might end up back on our doorstep. But when I thought about it really hard, I realized that I didn't want her back. I wanted my family back, but that's not a good enough reason to have someone in your life. She probably figured that out, too. Or maybe it was something else; I don't know. I wasn't the perfect partner to her; I know that. But I didn't think there was any point in confessing my infidelity, especially when she was working on getting better. It would have felt like I was hurting her just to be vindictive and that didn't make sense. So my secret stayed with me.

We talk of course. We have to for Emily's sake but we've never gone back to the way it was before. She only came close once.

We were having our usual weekly call. As planned, Emily spent summers with her mother on the west coast of Canada, and came back to me at the end of August to continue school in Kilmarnock. Her mother was missing her; I could tell. "I want to thank you for everything, Malcolm. I didn't want her to go back; I was hoping she'd stay in Canada. Some days it feels almost unnatural that she isn't with me…" There's silence on the other end of the line for a moment before she continues, "but I can't keep her. I should have known that."

"We'd be lost without her. I couldn't wait for her to get back." It was true. And I wasn't entirely sure she'd come back to us either. She told me she was returning and she kept talking about it when she talked to me or my dad or Hardly on the phone but until she got off that plane, I didn't know for sure.

"It's not just that. I want to thank you for everything." The line goes very quiet before she continues. "For all of it."

That's when I knew for sure. She had started over again, and she wasn't coming back. Maybe we do end up with our mothers.

"It's okay. I know."

She got better or at least the problems she had became manageable. She changed doctors three times and her new doctor changed her diagnosis from bipolar disorder to post-traumatic stress disorder. The doctor thought her mood swings and dark days were linked to what happened to her as a child. I don't know which doctor was right and I don't think it mattered. She found out what was required to control her affliction and she did what she needed to do. And she followed through on her dream. She used the money she inherited to start a fund for young girls who got into trouble. She works at it harder than anything she's ever done. Early on she tried to send money but I wouldn't let her. Then she said it was for Emily so we put it in an account. And then one day I noticed a positive balance on my bank account, for a large amount. I thanked her and I accepted it. And I asked her to not do it again. I use it when I take time away from work to travel with Emily or my father. And when our old clunker started giving us problems and we needed to buy a newer car, it was nice to be able to get a vehicle that we really wanted.

When it came time to choose a university, Emily decided she was best suited to stay close to home so she picked the University of Glasgow. Her mother helped her purchase her own car and she drove from Kilmarnock to school most days. We couldn't have been prouder of her – all of us.

Life became life. I saw Nan once or twice when I was out running and we waved but we never spoke. I understand now what she meant when she told me that we should take our pleasures where we can. I take my pleasures from my relationships with Emily and Hardly, and even Terry and Jo. They came to visit for two weeks before Emily started university, and I got to show them the Scotland that I couldn't adequately describe when we talked on our computers. And I got to be a son to my father, the type of son he deserved. When his health deteriorated, it wasn't connected to his memory problem. That was dementia. Just as Heather's affliction was diagnosed, so was my dad's. He was given medication to deal with it, but it doesn't go away. His brain just kept eating away at itself and it got worse and worse. As long as he kept to his routine, the confusion he experienced was minimized but if we took him out of his environment then he'd invariably have a slip. We'd see it in his face or he'd repeat the same questions or statements even more frequently than when he was first diagnosed. He was destined to reach a point where he wouldn't know where he was and who we were; that's the way the disease works. We never got to that point though, and perhaps that was for the best. When the doctor took us aside at the hospital and told us it was his heart, I didn't believe him. I've never known anyone who has a bigger, stronger heart than my dad. The doctor said he'd probably had four or five heart attacks previously but he just kept right on moving along, not acknowledging them. Then one day he had a pain in his chest when he was up on a ladder cleaning out the gutters at a neighbor's house. We spent four days in the hospital with him and each day he got a little bit worse.

Last night he spoke to me. I know he did. Everyone went for a break and left us alone. His eyes were closed and the machine was letting out its short, little beats. I closed my eyes for a moment and I heard his voice. It was steady, the way it used to be, and he spoke as though we were in the middle of a long conversation.

"The old things that you remember – when you touch them again after many, many years, a feeling comes over you. It can be a person that you touch, sometimes it is a person, or sometimes it can be a thing, and it takes you back. It touches you inside, son, and you remember. And if you're lucky you feel different."

I don't hear the beeps of the machine or the little tufts of breaths. I keep waiting for him to take a breath or stop, but he keeps talking and I keep my eyes tightly shut. "That's what this is about, Malcolm. That's all that this is about. These things last. You might not think they do, but they do. They're forever."

When I open my eyes, he's quiet, his eyes are closed and the machine continues to emit its steady, little sounds.

Hardly is talking to him now. I don't think my dad can see him but he can hear him. I know he can. I go over to Emily's side and she makes way for me. I lean forward and I smell his smell, the same smell that taught me, raised me, loved me. For the first time in three days, real, actual words come out. When he speaks, he barely makes a sound and his lips struggle as they part and seal again.

"Still time. Lots of time."

For one, brief moment, he's with us. He smiles his dad smile and his eyes stay in one place. And then he leaves me. He leaves all of us. I squeeze his hand, trying to bring him back, but there is no reaction. I call for the nurse, the doctor, anyone, but it's no use. Emily's arms are around my waist, holding me tight. I shake and then I vibrate. I push her away but she follows and drapes her body around mine, squeezing me with every bit of strength she can muster. She's holding on to save herself as well as to save me. Hardly is on the other side of the bed, still speaking, not quite believing it yet, whispering something to my father, his father, our father. He leans forward and kisses his forehead and I hear him say, "Thank you".

It's too much. I kiss Emily on the forehead and then gently release her to Flora, who's standing quietly by the door. I go to my friend and stand beside him, the same way I did so many years ago when we walked to school together. He stands up and the strong, little man embraces me. We don't need to speak. We know. We both know. A great man died right in front of us and the world is not quite as right as it was before.

Chapter Twenty-Four

IT WAS A tragic time but we got through it. Even my mother telephoned. She wanted to come to Scotland to pay her respects, but I asked her not to. He would have preferred it that way.

And now he's with us every day. I feel his hand on my shoulder when I struggle with a decision, and I see the beginnings of his crinkled smile on my face when I look in the mirror. Emily is no longer a child. Her initial studies to become a historian didn't work out. Maybe part of that had been to please her grandfather, I don't know. She's an artist now. She earns her living arranging living rooms and houses for people with too much money and she paints amazing, colorful images on huge canvasses in her spare time. The orange and blue walls of her first Kilmarnock bedroom must have inspired her. When she visits me, she becomes a little girl again. She calls me Daddy and spends time with her, still improperly pronounced, Uncle Harry. She has her mother's independence and my father's strength of character, and perhaps there's a little bit of me in there, too. And, I finally took her advice; I have a lady of my own these days. Mary drifted into my life a few months after Dad passed. We met at the library, the grand, old Dick Institute, when I was returning some books. She isn't a school teacher, she's a writer. She was reading from one of her novels to a group of people, and I couldn't stop watching her. From there we became friends and today we're a little more than friends. Mary feels things; she has empathy. She seems to know when I'm hurting or feeling a little off and she comes to me, and I do the same for her. I don't know where we're going or what's going to happen but we enjoy our time together, and that's enough for now.

We heard from Heather shortly after we lost Dad, and she said she'd come out and help if we needed her. She didn't want to, though. Emily and I knew that so we politely declined. Her life is busy now. You'll see her if you ever find yourself in downtown Vancouver, on the west coast of Canada, handing out food or blankets to homeless people. Emily tells me that she fights bureaucracy during the day trying to raise funds for women who are in need, and at night she walks the streets with a group of volunteers as they counsel and help less fortunate souls. She still has her inconsistent times but she sounds happy and she tells Emily that she hasn't heard the sounds of ghosts in many years.

And Hardly got his very own romance. Flora and he made it; they even got married. He collects a medallion once a year on his sobriety date from the funny meetings that he didn't want to go back to. He has eight of them now and when Flora started accompanying him, she decided she had the same problem that he has. She has six medallions of her own, sneaking right up behind him.

Two years after Dad passed, Emily got us all together and insisted that we take a trip up to Aberdeen. There was a castle she wanted to see again.

"Dad, Mary, and Uncle Harry, listen to me. You, too Flora; don't laugh. There are no double-paned windows in this castle. It has not been rebuilt; it's still in its original state of ruins. It's very important that you come and see it."

I speak to no one in particular. "I remember taking you there."

She turns and smiles for me, and only me, before continuing. "We should all see it. It's the perfect time of year."

Hardly will do anything for her. She knows this. "Cold, miserable and wet. Yes, perfect, love. When do we leave?"

We make the trip up north in my vehicle, driving through the fog to get there. We walk the trail up to the old castle as Emily tells Flora about a movie that was shot here years ago. The light is beginning to come over the old ruin. Mary is in the middle between my daughter and my best friend and his wife. She looks back to check on me but I wave her ahead, feigning that I'm tired from the long drive.

As they turn the corner, the sun shines over the top walls of the castle and it is indeed majestic. The bright, yellow light hits me square in the eyes and I feel my father. I feel everything he was, and I feel everything that ever happened in my life. Emily and Hardly's voices call back, telling me to hurry, and I realize what he was trying to say to me. None of it is ever temporary. Living is what matters. You take from your life what you can. There are times when you stand defiantly at the edge of the cliff and feel the spray from the ocean hitting you in the face, and there are times when you're falling from the sky and you're all alone. You feel all of them, and some of them hurt, but they all matter, and you still have to live. You have to participate in life.

My face is wet with emotion but I don't care. I turn the corner and all of them are waiting for me. My tears don't surprise them. Mary comes to me but Emily holds herself back. They know.

Emily leads us over to her favorite place. She stands in front of a small cluster of standing stones. Flora and Mary stand away from us and huddle together. They might be shielding each other from the cold, or it's more likely that they're giving the three of us a minute together. Hardly teeters slightly, as he leans his weight on his cane, and then against me, as we stand in front of Emily.

The clouds suddenly close together, blocking the sun. It's getting darker. We all know what's coming. Emily looks up to the sky, anticipating the rain. Then she puts her fingers to her lips and for just a moment she's a little girl again. "Shhh, the spirits are talking to us."

She waits and waits. She has her own thoughts, her own memories, and I know somewhere in there she's thinking about my dad, her grandfather. When she speaks, she looks only at me, speaking slowly and strongly, ignoring the tears in her eyes. "It's all right. The spirits say we're going to be okay. Everything is going to be okay."

Then she smiles and I realize that she's right. This is all I need. It's all I've ever needed.

Other Martin Crosbie books:

My Temporary Life is Book One of the My Temporary Life trilogy. Available here: http://amzn.to/2i4cbJJ.

My Name is Hardly is Book Two of the My Temporary Life trilogy. Available here: http://amzn.to/2gPRjEP.

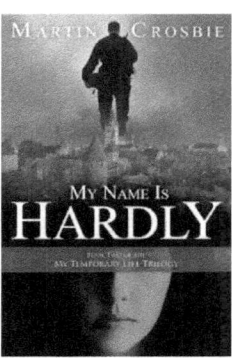

All Good Men Must Fall is Book Three of the My Temporary Life trilogy. Available here: http://amzn.to/2mTY2Eo

Believing Again: A Tale of Two Christmases is available here: http://amzn.to/2hWZUe5.

The Dead List: A John Drake Mystery is available here:
http://amzn.to/2hJt90L.

Lies I Never Told: A Collection of Short Stories is available here:
http://amzn.to/2gZMmNg.

How I Sold 30,000 eBooks on Amazon's Kindle—An Easy-To-Follow Self-Publishing Guidebook is available here: http://amzn.to/2hJBFPO.

In a year-end press release, Amazon called Martin Crosbie's debut novel *My Temporary Life* one of their success stories. His bestselling work has been lauded in *Publisher's Weekly*, *Forbes*, and Canada's *Globe and Mail* newspaper. Martin's recent release *The Dead List (A John Drake Mystery)* was awarded a publishing contract by Kindle Press.

Martin was born in the Highlands of Scotland and currently makes his home just outside Vancouver, on the west coast of Canada.

Martin enjoys hearing from his readers at martin@martincrosbie.com. Or you can sign up for his newsletter here http://martincrosbie.com/bookdoggy-newsletter-sign-up/.

https://twitter.com/Martinthewriter
https://www.facebook.com/martin.crosbie.3
http://martincrosbie.com/